# My Ridiculous, Romantic Obsessions

OTHER BOOKS BY BECCA WILHITE

*Bright Blue Miracle*

# *Chapter One*

**M**om pulls her new toy, a talking GPS directions-thingie up close to her eyes. "Turn right here. No, here. Sarah, you missed it. Now Mildred's recalibrating." I swear if I hear the polite, British GPS voice—which, yes, Mom named—tell me one more time that she's recalibrating, I'll chuck her right out the window.

"It's okay, Mom. There's another entrance to the parking lot." I point ahead half a block and turn into the lot between two huge trees. *It's almost over,* I tell myself. *And then somehow you'll miss this.*

*Try me,* I respond.

This drive to school, the big drop-off, is reminiscent of home life in ridiculous ways. Mom tells me she wants me to drive, to try out her new car. Then she hovers around, watching to see if my hands are at ten and two, telling me I'm turning on my blinker too soon, bracing with her arms every time I tap the break. And Dad sits in the backseat with a magazine on his lap.

"Hey, Dad. We're here," I tell him. His head jerks up, and he looks momentarily confused. He must have been sleeping

1

through Mom and Mildred's directional play-by-play. I can't blame him. I'd have liked to be sleeping, too. I guess I will be tonight, right here in my first apartment.

I look up at the unimpressive three-story tan brick buildings surrounded by metal railings that are peeling white flecks of paint. I hope my room has a window. It has to, right? Fire code and stuff?

Pulling into an empty parking slot, I pull on the brake and watch Mom, bent in half, picking stuff up off the floor of the car. She hands me my purse and the apartment key and then leans over me to pop the back hatch.

She's excited for me to move into this next stage of my life.

She and Dad jump out of the car and sling my suitcases and two boxes of kitchen stuff onto the sidewalk.

"Do you need help getting this inside?" Dad asks. What a silly question. Of course I want him to carry my bags in.

"What a silly question. Of course she doesn't want us to hang around here." Mom grins at him and swats his arm. "Bye, sweetie," she says. "Be good," she sort of chirps at me as she squeezes my shoulders and runs for the car door.

Dad looks like he's still waking up.

"Why don't you come inside, and I'll get you a drink of something." I glance at my kitchen box, which has nothing drinkable in it, unless you count that Mexican vanilla I've been saving.

"Nah, honey. Mom's right. We should get out of here and let you move in without us bothering you." He says it with a smile, all happy Dad-style, so why does it sting? I shrug.

Mom leans her head out the window. "Okay, well, bye! Time for us to go!" She has a little manic touch to her singing tone, and she's pointing to her watch.

"Please come in for a few minutes. Maybe we'll meet my roommates." I go for the social angle. This one works every time.

"I'm sorry, Sarah. We've got a plane to catch," Dad says.

I know I heard that wrong. A plane? My parents don't go anywhere.

"What?" My head is trying to explode.

"We can't be late. Wouldn't want that ship to leave without us!" Dad's using his too-cheery Santa voice. Plane? Ship?

Mom giggles out her window. "We wanted to surprise you. You're starting a new life. And so are we." She's showing all her teeth. "We're heading out this afternoon for a cruise. To St. Maarten! Can you believe it?"

No.

I can't believe it.

"Um."

"Fun, right?" Dad asks. I nod, unable to produce words. My smile feels lopsided and fake.

Dad side-arm hugs me again, tucks a fifty-dollar bill into my hand (for groceries, until I get a job), and somehow slips in behind the wheel before I find my voice. I step over to his open window. "So I have that long weekend next month. Are you going to come pick me up, or should I"—shudder—"catch a bus home?"

Dad rubs at an invisible spot on the windshield. Mom giggles. Again.

"Actually, sweetie, that won't work, because we're spending that weekend on the houseboat with Aunt Melanie. We've had it planned for months—can't get out of it now. So enjoy your freedom," she proclaims. Really, she proclaims it. With a hand flourish for a bonus.

And then the car is pulling out of the parking lot, narrowly missing my toes as I stand there with my mouth open.

*Enjoy your freedom.* Yeah, I guess. Looks like Mom is taking her own advice.

Okay, so there's something we need to get straight here. Even with parents like that, I am a totally normal girl. I'm not psychotic, and I've never been very neurotic, although the events of the drop-off could change that. I may have a few dramatic tendencies, but they are tucked back behind my very correct behavior.

For instance, I may have a habit of talking to myself. Mostly not out loud. But sometimes I also answer, and usually it's in a British accent. That's not too weird, except that lately, it sounds a lot like the voice of Mildred the GPS. And if, let's say just hypothetically, I happened to have read through a few too many thrilling romance novels where the ladies have long flowing gowns to match their long flowing hair and long flowing names, that doesn't mean I think life is going to follow that sort of story.

I know the formula—he wants her, she refuses him, he charms her, she holds her ground, he does something dramatic like saves her from a fire or reinstates her family's lost fortune or dies, she realizes she loved him all along, wedding bells ring or pirate flags unfurl or she joins a convent, happily ever after— but I don't expect to live that way. I've learned that life is not like novels. Especially not like novels with rippling muscles on paperback covers.

After reading a couple hundred of those books—you know, hypothetically speaking—you start to see that there's not that much difference between a romance and an epic fantasy. You've got your quest, sometimes it involves a ring, and a hero who will stop at nothing to do what he has to. The difference is usually the girl.

And I'm not that girl.

I'm not the girl who inspires men to commit acts of heroism. In real life, those girls speak much more quietly and breathe a lot louder than I do. I'm not the girl who strikes men speechless with her beauty. Really, really not. I don't even know how to flutter my eyelashes. But that's life. Not romance-novel life, just real life.

Life is like this: You get what you deserve. You find your place, and you stay in it. And you hope to have something gorgeous to look at once in a while. This is why I came to school to study art history. Because I like having gorgeous things to look at. And I like paintings and sculpture too.

Here's what happened. My friend Chel left for the university a semester early. She's not a genius or anything. She's not even as smart as I am. But her parents are planners, and with their gentle nudges (that left bruises), she finished high school early and got a head start on college classes.

During her first semester, she took an introduction to art history class. And there was this guy. He was the teacher assistant, and he was beautiful. She would go to study sessions and take pictures of him by holding her phone under the table. Those pictures were enough to convince me to come to school here.

If there were real, human guys that looked like that, well, you could count me in.

So now it's my first semester and here I am in Dr. Novetsky's History of Western Art (Monday/Wednesday/Friday at 9:00 A.M.). It's a biggish-sized class, about a hundred kids. Dr. Novetsky treats her classroom like a battlefield. Vampire-like, she sucks all the enjoyment out of beautiful paintings, music, buildings, and sculpture, scattering dates, numbers, categories, and lists in her wake. The course fulfills a general requirement. That explains all the students here. But the fact that she doesn't scare every person right out of the art history major is due mainly to her remarkable teacher assistant.

Remarkable in his hotness. There he sits in his Iranian glory (black hair, heavy brows over dark chocolate eyes, lips you just want to put your fingers on), slouched in a chair at the front of the auditorium. As Novetsky plows through images projected from her laptop, he watches over the class like a Middle Eastern god. (Except that I hear he's from exotic St. Paul. But who am I to ruin the mystique?)

It doesn't take long to weigh the pros and cons. The first lecture is concise and heartless. We will study art because it is Essential. Because it is Important. Because it is Required. But not, by any means, because we expect to enjoy it. There will be no fun here. At the same time as my heart and soul are shriveling, I stare at the TA and realize that this could be one of those opportunities to find my own "worthwhile"—I can still love the works of the masters in spite of Vampire Professor. As long as I keep watching the TA.

Casually taking notes through the second lecture, I spend equal time glancing between the projected images and the god-like guy in front of the theater. I wonder if I could ever, under any circumstances, speak to him. Not likely. Too bad, really, but knowing me, I am satisfied to simply sit and stare. And fantasize. A totally chaste fantasy that involves bringing him to my apartment, putting him up on the wall like my very own piece of fine art, gazing at him at regular intervals, and occasionally passing near enough to touch his mouth. As long as I can see him, I can insert his face onto any over-described romance hero.

He doesn't even flinch as Novetsky tells the class there will be a "heavy quiz" every Monday morning in class. (Note to self: Get that woman a copy of *How to Win Friends and Influence People*.)

As Novetsky's lecture ends and the room starts disgorging students, I hear a voice from behind me in the theater. "I could use a study group. Who's in?" Waving my hand as I put my laptop in my bag, I turn around and see the greatest face—even better than the amazing TA—attached to a tall, broad-shouldered guy.

*Oh, please. I don't deserve this, but please. Just for a few hours a week. Please.*

In a romance novel, he'd be the underprivileged farm worker whose heart is almost as large as his rippling pectorals. His straw-colored hair would fall over his tanned, intense forehead as he leans across a ravine to rescue a stray lamb. He's perfect because he looks like a real person. But hotter.

He's looking at me. Coming from art history territory, I notice that he's got this unbelievably chiseled jawbone—an Adonis face the masters would love to sculpt. And he's smiling. At me. I've suddenly forgotten why I am here.

For several long seconds I stare at his hazel eyes and forget to care why I am here. I watch him shoulder his bag with easy confidence and I no longer know where "here" is. He glances around and looks back at me and tosses out his magnificent smile and I'm not at all sure about the whole time and space and relativity business. I remind myself to breathe before I collapse.

That is when I remember Chel's warning that I should wear better clothes to class. She's told me for years that someday I'll regret the T-shirt and yoga pants look. This is probably that day. *Oh, well,* I think. *I'll be the brains. He can be the looks.* Except it's possible I say that out loud. But not very loud. Maybe he can't hear me over all the exit noises. I've got to cover up.

"Study group?" I manage to stammer.

He says, "You're in? Great." He leans close to my head and whispers, "You can be the brains." He grins this slightly crooked smile, and I feel my head steaming.

Can I even smile back at him? I try, but it feels terrible. Too much teeth, not enough confidence. Story of my life.

The slouching kid beside Adonis stands hunched over his phone, ready to collect stats. It looks like he's playing secretary. "Quizzes on Mondays. So study group—when? Sunday?" His voice doesn't move. He sounds either bored or depressed.

A cute girl leans over and shakes her head. I'm relieved that she's only cute in a small, harmless, chipmunk-ish sort of way. That means less competition, and she's not likely to play those stupid, elegant-girl games. You know, where the girl talks all breathy and either fakes being smarter than she is or dumber than she is. Chipmunk Girl says, "I go home Sundays. What about Saturday mornings?"

"No good." Adonis shakes his head. He and Slouch look at each other. "Tutoring," they both say.

He tutors? That is so attractive. Tall, hot, and smart? I believe they call that a triple threat.

"Fridays, then? After classes?" Chipmunk asks.

Nods, all around.

"Okay," Slouch says in a defeated voice. "Hit me. Names and numbers."

That poor guy wouldn't even make it into a romance novel. Maybe, *maybe* if he was lucky he could be the preacher's assistant who either faithfully guards delicate family secrets or treacherously leaks sordid information to the townsfolk. But he shouldn't count on it. He's just not romance material.

I wait for Adonis to report his vitals, but it looks like Slouch already knows him. Right. Tutoring together. Lucky him. Slouch looks over at me.

"I'm Sarah." As I give him my number, I notice Adonis thumbing his phone. Is he keying in my number? Is he writing me in? Am I being *added?*

"How do you spell that?" Adonis asks.

I am *so* being added. Slouch doesn't seem to notice, so I give my attention to Adonis. As if I had any choice.

"With an H. With two, actually. My last name is Hastings." Why? Why do I always give too much information? No heroine in any romance novel worth its newsprint would volunteer so much detail. *Sarah, darling, no one cares. Least of all Adonis, here.*

He looks a little confused. "With an H?"

"Yeah, you know, at the end." I'm either going to laugh or vomit, so I laugh. "S-A-R-A-H."

He must be an old-school gentleman, because he's keying it all in. On some visceral level, I am pleased. Then I wage a war across the two sides of my brain—the logical versus the psychotic.

*There is absolutely no chance in the real world that this person will call.*

*He just took the number, didn't he? He's clearly been raised correctly.*

*A gentleman's reaction. Zero chance of a call.*

*First and last names—all in the phone.*

*He will never, ever remember me. Hey, wait. What is he doing with his phone?*

*Ha! He's snapping a picture so he will always, always remember me.*

*You psycho. I don't want anyone to remember me.*

*Are you kidding? He's a Greek god. Chiseled from stone. He could be Our Hero.*

*You're nuts. Stop distracting me. You make it very difficult to remain focused.*

*That's not me, sweetie. That's Adonis.*

"What are you doing?" I sound like a person in a panic. But I am, after all, a person in a panic. I mean, really. Photos?

"I'm terrible with names. Do you mind if I put your face in there? And your hair? I'm probably not going to forget that hair."

Ugh. My hair. Wild, ferocious curls ringing my head like Medusa. The kind of hair that makes it into a romance novel on the head of the well-meaning but scatterbrained friend, or the wild little sister. Do I mind? If I did mind, it's too late now. And speaking of late, I've got another class.

"Okay, well. See you all later," I mutter to the room at large and escape toward the door and the safety of philosophy—a small class without any romance novel possibilities.

⁓

What do you expect to hear in a classroom discussion in Philosophy 102? I'm thinking maybe a little Plato, a little Hobbes, a little Socrates. I hadn't counted on Existential Journey Girl.

We are in the middle of the second lecture when a girl comes striding in to class. She doesn't glide in as though propelled by the air in her head; she doesn't stomp like an angry kid. She moves with confidence as she introduces herself and informs Dr. Younger that she will be adding this course.

As she sits down I get a good look at her. Spiky blonde hair, intelligent face, and she accessorizes like Chel. I think her clothes are stylish, but really, what do I know? She looks well-put-together, anyway, and I'm thinking we could be friends. Until she raises her hand to speak.

All her appealing confidence seems to drip out her elbow as she waves a floppy arm. Glazed dullness covers her eyes and her whole face goes soft. Her voice, when she speaks, has lost its commanding edge.

"Which philosophers dealt with dreams? Because that's what I need to discover from this class experience," she says in a breathy, limp voice.

My stomach clenches in visceral reaction. Oh. She's one of them—those horrible girls who practically pant when they speak in front of guys, forcing the guys to lean in closer and ditch their girlfriends.

Dr. Younger's reaction is almost quick enough to be natural. "My Web page outlines the course aims clearly. We're going over the basics of Greek culture today."

As though she hears words the rest of us can't, she responds in her airy voice, "Oh, good. I have a vital connection with my dreams. The Universe speaks to me as I sleep, guiding me on my soul's journey." She capitalizes Universe when she says it.

Without moving my head, I glance around to see if I'm the only one repulsed by this. She's such a faker. Only minutes have passed since she introduced herself like a totally normal person in a totally normal voice. Now she's turned into something mysterious and whispery. A guy wearing a Van Halen T-shirt is

11

staring, open-mouthed, as if waiting for her to drop something so he can pick it up for her. Ick. There is a small explosion of air behind me as someone tries to stifle a laugh. Two girls on the side of the room have their heads together.

Maybe everyone knew girls like this in high school. The girls who work so hard to appear innocent and sweet, who pretend to be sincere but refuse to use their minds in front of guys. And the voice—it's always that breathy, come-closer-to-hear-me voice. I hate girls like that; one girl in particular. But guys seem to love them. Why is that? Seriously, what is attractive about that? Isn't there a guy out there who could find brains beautiful? It's like these girls are sure whoever they are isn't going to catch a man so they'll pretend to be someone else. And then they catch the man. It does seem to work, I'll give them that.

Dr. Younger stares at the girl, maybe waiting to see if she's going to tie her little monologue into his lecture. Poor guy. I haven't felt sorry for him before this moment. He seems to love his subject, and he's a capable teacher. He's got his class under control and gave us a great introductory lecture. And here he stands, looking stunned.

"Last night I *dreamt*"—she says it British-style—"that all my skin was missing. I was experiencing the world through raw nerves. The Universe is telling me to remove all my defenses and allow the World Soul to touch me in places no one has ever been." Her eyes flutter like a hypnotized person and she touches her face.

I feel my skin crawl with every fake word she says. I glance around again and see that several guys are leaning forward. Actually moving their bodies toward her. Ack.

Dr. Younger blinks himself into polite command of the class. "Thank you for sharing with us. When you have spent some time studying the class materials, you will be able to recognize how all aspects of living are rationally and causally interrelated."

Back on track, Dr. Younger proceeds with his lecture. I type in the notes, letting half my mind wander as he speaks.

*I wonder if he's related to Cole Younger.*

*The bandit?*

*I prefer "outlaw"—and he preferred "freedom fighter."*

*I'm sure we're not going to have this discussion again. The gang is dead. They do not need your validation, or your dodgy public defender's justification. Nobody alive really cares about the old American outlaws anymore.*

*I'm not justifying anyone. I'm just saying that they were all led astray by the nefarious Jesse James.*

Have I mentioned that I hate Jesse James? While there are a few American outlaws who I tolerate, and a couple whom I admire (okay, really only Butch Cassidy, and he's always wearing Paul Newman's face), Jesse James is nothing but wickedness incarnate. And it probably has nothing to do with a certain string of events in my high school career involving a guy named Jesse. Or with the humiliation connected to that string of events. But my humiliation-turned-vengeance did earn me a great grade on a term paper in my honors American history class, even though I understand perfectly well that the wrong Jesse was nailed to the wall. Let's just say that Jesse James the outlaw has never figured into any of my personal romance fantasies, and he never will. And no one else named Jesse will either, ever again.

⌒

The weekend before classes started, while my parents were cruising the Caribbean, I found a great job proofreading for the university's online learning department. So Tuesdays and Thursdays I get to spend the hours from noon to four tucked away inside a cubicle with three other girls and a guy named Dean, the token male proofreader. We shuffle paper (yeah, I know about the trees, but trust me, it's better to proofread a paper copy than go blind staring at a monitor all afternoon) and snicker at the professors' ridiculous grammar.

If I were the type to categorize people (heaven forbid), here's how the afternoon proofers would shake out: Maura is the Goth holdout, complete with dyed black eyebrows and purple lipstick. Tandy is the comic relief. She even looks like a clown (but a very cute one) with her long, skinny body, big feet, and round red nose. Okay, just kidding about the nose part. Shari is the nerd— and yes, I know that sounds mean. Let me clarify that there's nothing wrong with being the nerd, and I'm glad it's her. If she weren't here, it would be me. We use Shari in place of reference material. Dean is quiet, efficient, and totally overwhelmed by the estrogen content of our shared cubicle.

And I'm the normal one.

Thursday afternoon we stand around the vending machine on our enforced break. Our supervisor (who doesn't want us to call her "our boss" because her name is actually Vickie Boss) insists we take this ten-minute breather for our mental stability. It's pretty nice of her, but I think there's more to it than that. And I'm not the only suspicious proofreader in the group.

"So why does the Boss kick us out of the cube every after-noon at two? What is she doing that she doesn't want us to see?" Tandy asks in a super-secret-agent voice while she rubs her hands together. "Oh, I know. Maybe she's involved in an international spy ring, and she has to hit the dead letter drop every afternoon, and she's making sure none of us see the spot, and—wait for it—she has to do it faithfully, every day, because the fate of the free world rests on her shoulders!"

Laughing, Shari says, "Try a little realistic." Her twisted grammar surprises and pleases me.

Maura rolls her heavily lined eyes. "She probably just needs a smoke and doesn't want to corrupt us."

Dean shakes his head. "She doesn't smoke." We all wait to hear how he could know something like that already. "I worked here all summer, and I know who the smokers are. She's not one of them." We look at him for more ideas, but he isn't really interested in making a suggestion, just defending the Boss.

"Maybe," I suggest, "she's on the phone to a call-in radio show. Like with a hack psychologist who will tell her how to save her marriage."

Dean shakes again. "She's not married."

I'm feeling annoyed with him now. Doesn't this boy know how to play gossip games? "Then maybe she's trying to save her divorce," I shoot back. At least he smiles.

There are certain parts of a girl's life that are planned out and organized. Things set just how they should be. Take that first college apartment, for example. I'd pretty much assumed I'd be sharing a place with Chel and we'd have, between us, great food and great clothes and there would be a party every night.

Not so much. Chel ended up loving the house where she'd rented a room, so now I'm in a clean-but-shabby second-floor walk-up with two girls I didn't know last week. Lauren and Mandy. They don't speak, at least not to me. Lauren doesn't have anything to say, and Mandy's occupied. Her face is always stuck to her boyfriend. When I say always, I mean really, really always. I'm not entirely sure I could identify her in a lineup, unless I could look at the back of her head. Even then I think I'd need the boyfriend's hands on her hair to be absolutely certain.

When I get back to the apartment after work, I consider maybe doing homework in the front room, but it's taken. The back of Mandy's head signals that the front part is busy, possibly for the rest of the night. She pulls out an arm and waves at me as I walk through to my room. I think about waving back, but who would see it?

For a minute, I almost miss home, where no matter how strange my parents are, at least they speak to me. Sure, they say dumb things, guaranteed to come up at some future therapy session where I delve into my insecurities, but at least they speak.

Come to think of it, maybe I don't mind the silence.

## Chapter Two

On my way to art history Friday morning, I hear my phone chirping. It's not a number I recognize. As I'm deciding whether to answer, it stops ringing, and I hear a man-voice call out my name. I look up from the phone and see Adonis, stashing his phone in a pocket. If I tell you that the sun was shining behind his head framing him in a halo of light, you'll think I'm lying. But I'm not.

*Breathe now, please. No passing out between buildings.*

"Hey, Sarah. Wait up," he calls.

As though my feet weren't cemented to the sidewalk. Maybe he's calling a different Sarah. There must be a hundred of us out here during class break. I'll just stand here and see which girl he ends up talking to. I won't let my expectation grow too much, so I won't feel disappointed when she's someone else. I try to find something to focus on—a reason to have stopped walking. I decide on my phone, which I find is still in my hand. I would so love to appear nonchalant, but I think I may be staring at him with my mouth open. He walks right up to me. He's standing less than a foot away from me and giving me his full attention. I think it's me he's looking for.

"Remember me from art history? I was just calling you to see if you were going to class today."

Ah. That explains it all. He wants to ditch, but knows that without notes, he'll bomb the quiz on Monday. I am used to this by now. Guys may not want me, but they need me for my brains. And not just the infamous Jesse James. Lots of guys decide that they need my company if there's homework to be done. Were I a woman of character, I would surely refuse to give him my notes. Turns out I have no character at all.

"Yeah, I'm on my way. Do you want me to get notes for you?" Wow, he's tall. And he's standing very close. Looking a little confused.

"No, I'm coming too. But," now he's smiling, "if you let me sit with you, I promise not to copy all your notes. Just half of them." He nudges me with an elbow. Physical contact. Chel will need details. Not that I'm likely to forget about this.

We wander into Novetsky's theater and find two seats together. I stare at the projector, waiting for the lights to go out, because I'm unable to think of a single thing to say to Adonis. Eventually the room dims and the projector starts up. At this point I realize that there were probably at least seven different openings for me to discover Adonis's name. Would it have killed me to try to speak to him? Um, yeah. Probably. After the first few slides, I realize I can hear myself breathing. Can he hear that?

With half my brain I absorb Professor Novetsky's heartless lecture. The other half is whirring, trying to figure out how to get this guy's name without sounding like a total moron. He knows my name, so the time for introductions has clearly passed. I'm not sure he'd love being referred to as Adonis, although I can't really imagine why he'd object. Some people are funny like that.

Only at the end of the lecture do I even glance down at the godlike TA. Yes, he's still here. Yes, he still appears to be breathing in and out. Yes, he has maintained his physical perfection. So why haven't I been staring all through class?

"Study group tonight at Caleb's, right? How are you getting there?" Adonis asks.

Caleb? Is that Slouch's name? Wow. Adonis is good. And handsome. And intimidating. I can barely speak. "I'm not that far from his apartment. I think I'll walk over," I mumble into my bag.

"Do you think it's weird to have a study group on a Friday night?"

"Yeah, a little," I say. Now that I've started talking, I can't make myself shut up. "But six-thirty is early, so it leaves the night and the rest of the weekend to do whatever." He must be mentally juggling his social events calendar to fit us in, just to pass a Monday quiz. I wonder what he'll do after the study group. Who will be waiting for him?

There must be a leading lady in his life. She probably has silky hair and shy eyes. I wonder if she rides horses. Maybe she has a tragic past that he's saving her from. Instantly I fill in her details. Her name is at least three syllables long—preferably four. Something like Arabella or Bellissima or Cordelia or Diantha (yes, I could give you one for every letter—so what?).

"How about I walk over with you?" he asks.

What? Walk over where? Oh, to Slouch's apartment for study group. Right. That's what we were talking about. I'm finding it a little tricky to stay focused here.

"Why?" Did I just ask that? I am such an idiot. But I'd love to know what he wants. There must be something he wants. Guys like him don't walk around to study groups with girls like me. Ever.

He looks startled again. Then his face relaxes into amusement. He licks a finger and holds it up to test the wind inside the auditorium. "It's a nice day. And if I walk you there, I can walk you home after so you won't be alone in the dark."

After telling him where I live, I bolt outside and phone Chel. Her voice mail picks up on the first ring. I bark, "Six-eight-seven-six," our code for Must Talk Right Now. Before I make it to the philosophy lecture hall, she's called back.

"Hey. I got your message. Are you okay?"

"I'm good, but what does it mean if Adonis wants to walk me to study group?"

Chel breathes her patented pay-attention noise: a cross between a sigh and a huff. "Either he thinks you'll get lost and forget to bring all your great notes if he leaves you alone, or he likes you. If he likes you, he either wants to spend a few extra minutes with you, or he doesn't like the thought of you getting to that other guy's place before him."

I don't get it. "Why would he care?"

"Sweetie, he doesn't want to leave you alone with that depressed guy. Maybe he's afraid you'll be the one to cheer him up, if you know what I mean."

"Chel, you are so deluded. But thank you for thinking that. You are a generous individual." She's been generous with me for years. Sometimes I wonder why she puts up with my insecurities and my general cluelessness about guys. Then I remember that she can't cook and I can.

"So did you get his name?" she asks.

"Sheesh. No. I don't know how. He already has my name, phone number, and address. Somehow I missed the normal opportunity. Help."

"Leave it to me. I'll be over at your place when he comes to . . . Pick You Up." I can hear her eyebrows wiggling. Chel doesn't live in a romance novel. More like a detective story, one with shadowy corners and pools of yellow light.

"Thanks. See you tonight. Come early. I'll feed you," I offer.

"I'm totally counting on it. Bye."

A knock at the door. Chel shoves me to the sink. "You do dishes. I'll get all the goods."

I know I should feel like I'm getting the short end of this deal, but it's no use pretending that she's not awesome at this. She's just comfortable right away, even around beautiful men. I can hear the swish as she opens the door.

"Hey, is Sarah here?" It's Adonis. Hearing him say my name sends little prickles up the back of my neck.

Her: "She is. She's in the middle of something right now. Come on in. I'm Chel."

Him: "Hi, Chel. Ben."

Ben! A name. Ben. Okay, not bad. Especially if his last name is British and goes well with titles like "Lord" or "Duke" or "Captain."

Her: "So, Ben, where are you from?"

Is he going to tell her about his ancestral estate in Scotland? His horse-breeding farm in Morocco?

Him: "Here. My family lives outside of town. My dad works in administration here at the school."

Totally not romantic, but possibly handy.

Her: "Excellent. Can he get me a scholarship?"

Is she flirting with him? She's flirting, isn't she? If she is, he's a goner and I have absolutely no chance of getting him to even read my notes—ever again.

Him (laughing): "I hope not. He couldn't get me one."

Okay. Having too much fun without me. I toss the rest of the dishes in the sink and poke my head around the corner, hoping that she's not touching him. If she's touching him, she'll never eat in my apartment again.

He stands as I come in. This brings an eyebrow raise from Chel. Now she'll have to trust me that he's a gentleman.

"Hi, Sarah."

I'm going to do it. I'm going to say his name. I'm going to speak it aloud for the first time. With a smile of someone else's confidence, I open my mouth. "Hi, Adonis."

*Oh, you did not.*

*I think my ears are on fire.*

*You absolutely did not just call him Adonis.*

*Where is a very deep hole I can climb into?*

He is standing by the couch with a half-amused, half-confused look on his face. I mutter something about notes and bolt to my room. Could I lock myself in here and never, ever come out again? Chel could slide saucers full of smoothies and muffin crumbs under the door three times a day. Maybe I could scratch through the wallboards and make a passageway to the bathroom. I could pursue my education online and write journal articles under a pseudonym and wear dark colors and let my hair grow wild and hide in this room like a twenty-first century Emily Dickinson and never have to face Adonis or anyone else like him.

*We should probably stop referring to him that way. It might prevent embarrassing slipups.*

*Oh, shut up, you.*

Full disclosure: I make sure Ben sits first. (His name is Ben. Not Adonis, Ben. *Ben*.) Then I totally arrange not to be sitting beside him. Because I just walked next to him for thirteen and a half minutes on the way over here, and it's very hard to look at him from there. Next-to-and-below is not prime real estate. The advantage from that place is olfactory, not visual. He smells nice. Clean, like dryer sheets, which makes me wonder if he lives at home. His mom must do his laundry for him, because what guy thinks to buy dryer sheets?

But from there I can't really look at him. I tried, and it's like watching a movie from the front row. I'm just starting to feel good and dizzy when we make it to study group. He's been talking for the whole walk. Since I can't stare at his face, I watch his scuffed shoes and memorize sidewalk cracks to avoid humiliating trips and/or crashes. Would he be offended to know that I have no idea what he's saying? I like the sound of his voice, though, and if he can keep it up for seven blocks (up three, over four) I will not complain.

So here we sit around the table in Caleb's kitchen. Someone living in this apartment must have a girlfriend. There are artsy, framed prints on the walls, and curtains in the window. There's even a rug in the living room. I place myself directly across from Ben. That way I can casually look up from my laptop and gaze at his face. An excellent strategy. Except that it's not working. He's not staring purposefully at his notes, or at Caleb's screen full of Novetsky's slides, or at his own hands, or even at Chipmunk Girl. Every time I look up from my screen, he's looking my way. This will never do. Can teeth sweat?

My phone chirps. Text from Chel: HOW'S IT GOING?

Hands under the table, I respond: HE'S LOOKING @ ME.

MAYBE DINNER IN YR TEETH.

She thinks she's so funny. She's always trying to make me panic. Wait! Maybe there *is* dinner in my teeth. My heart starts to thud as I realize that I can't catch my reflection in my laptop. Maybe the back of my phone? Nope, too dark. I pick up a spoon lying on the table and hold it on my thigh. I very subtly glance into the back of it. Can't see much. Try again. I twist the spoon until I can see my teeth in the metal. They're reflected all bendy and huge—giant horse teeth between a tiny nose and a pygmy chin. I look like a freak, but I'm clean. No food flecks in the teeth.

The phone chirps again. Another text. But not from Chel.

WHT R U DOING OVR THR?

I meet his eyes this time. He's trying not to laugh at me. I am such an idiot.

MEMORIZATION TECHNIQUE, I send him.

SHOW ME?

I shake my head and toss my phone in the bag, steadying my breathing rate. Curse Chel and her stupid humor. It is time to start paying attention. Come on, Sarah. Greek crockery. Get into it.

## Chapter Three

Walking home with Ben . . . (Time out. Let's just take a second to enjoy the novelty of that phrase. *Walking home with Ben.* As in I Am Walking Home with Ben. If this moment were in a book, I'd be willowy and graceful, and he'd be smitten with my charm and dismayed at my appropriate distance. Things like this do not happen to me. Ever. I am not the girl who walks home with Ben. Or with anyone else, really. But for right now, I'm going to act like that girl. Okay, ready?) Walking home with Ben, I wonder if he's going to keep up a steady stream of chatter all the way back to my place. No such luck.

Looking down at the frizz that is my head, he shoves his hands in his pockets and breathes in the evening air. He nudges me with his elbow. I like that. "So I've been told I talk too much. You have now heard every interesting thing about me. It's your turn. Tell me something about you."

Oh, lovely. Apparently what I wasn't processing on the walk over tonight was the life story of this Greek god. Why couldn't I listen? Okay, I was listening, but not to his words so much.

More to the sound of his voice mixed with the wind in the trees . . . I am such a bozo. So what did he tell me? Something about his major? Family statistics? His favorite baseball team? What he does for fun? What he bought at the grocery store? His girlfriend, the runway model? I remember him saying he's the youngest in his family, but that doesn't mean he wants to know about mine, even if I wanted to open that bizarre can of worms. I even kind of remember him mentioning meeting Caleb the Slouch in some tutoring capacity, but then I zoned out while I imagined Ben as a tutor. Because if there's anything hotter than this guy, it's this guy plus brains.

"What do you want to know?" I'm trying for casual, but it sounds more like terrified.

"How about your middle name?"

"Jennie. With an I-E. It's my grandma's name." Too much information again. Keep it simple.

"What's your favorite animal?"

"Steak."

He laughs, loud and surprised. "Really? Steak?"

I shrug. I want to make him laugh again, but I'm at a total loss. No self-respecting romance heroine would have confessed to eating red meat, especially when that wasn't even the question. "What's yours?"

"I have a chocolate Lab."

Ouch. A dog guy. I once made a sacred oath that I would never date a dog guy. But I'm not dating anyone, am I? And chances are slim that I'll ever need to explain my pathetic and unromantic Dog Fear.

He goes on. "He's about a hundred years old. He sheds like a maniac. He has his own couch in the living room. He has arthritis and some kind of dog diabetes, and he spends most of his life watching television. My mom leaves the set on for him. When I was a kid, he slept in my bed. Under the covers. But now he doesn't really make it up the stairs anymore unless I carry him there, so I sleep alone."

Don't we all?

"What's his name?"

"Torpedo."

I probably shouldn't laugh, but considering what he just said, that's ironic.

"Hey, it wasn't always funny. He used to wait for me at the end of the driveway when the bus dropped me off. When I came around the corner he'd launch himself at me and knock me right over. I grew up with a constant bruise on the back of my head. When I got bigger, I learned to brace myself. He was great practice for football."

Hmm. Football is manly and dashing and athletic and totally not me.

"Did you play football in high school?"

"Yes. Right here at Central, remember?"

Rats. He must have said that, too. I laugh off my nerves.

He goes on, "But you are not talking about you. So I'm shutting up now to hear your stories."

"I don't have any stories," I sort of whine. I wish I didn't do that.

"What about Chel. Is she your roommate?"

"Nope. Best friend since high school. Chel has some stories," *which I am never going to tell you, because then you'd know that besides being petite and stylish, she is also witty and clever and adorable.* "She also has all the great qualities of a superior best friend. She loves good food, she's pretty smart, but not smarter than I am, and she has excellent fashion sense. This is helpful to me, as I have none. If not for Chel, I would dress like this all the time."

He's looking me over. I feel my neck start to heat up. "You look great like this," he says. He's playing the part of the romantic hero very nicely. Too bad he doesn't have the right female lead to play along with.

I pretend I didn't hear him. "And she is the queen of yummy-sounds. That's my favorite part of her."

"What's a yummy-sound?"

"You know, when you're eating something really tasty and you just kind of *mmm* or *ohhh* and close your eyes and live in that perfect moment? The rest of the world disappears for a minute. When I cook for Chel, she almost always does yummy-sounds."

"What do you cook?"

Does he really want me to tell him? A seasonal list of specialties? I guess he's just being polite. "Whatever I want to eat, I guess. Why? What do you cook?"

"I'm a pro if it comes in a can or a box. The easier the directions, the better. I once set my mom's kitchen curtains on fire making popcorn. In the microwave."

I laugh at him. Will he be offended? "You did not."

"I did. You know how it says right on the box that you're supposed to stay nearby? So you can listen for the popping to slow down? I didn't. And when I came back, flames. I opened the microwave and shoved the burning bag over to the sink. Right into a pan of water. The fire shot up to the curtains, and there was steam and smoke everywhere. The fire alarm started because the curtains were burning. Torpedo was leaping on me. It was bad. Scary. Long story short, I bought my mom some new curtains and I refuse to eat microwave popcorn ever again."

"Even if someone else does the hard part? The pushing buttons and removing before combustion?"

He shakes his head. "It's a mind game now. I just can't do it."

"So what do you eat when you just want a snack?"

"Chocolate chips, right out of the bag. And I've never met a candy bar I didn't like."

"Are you making this up? I've seen people who mainline chocolate and you don't look like they do." I think he's teasing me. He looks more like the type who goes running when he's hungry, to ward off the unhealthy sensation of wanting food.

"No kidding." He smiles. "Chocolate is my favorite food group. It's either a vegetable, because it comes out of a bean, or a fruit, because it grows on a tree. Either way, I feel very good about eating chocolate any time, any place. I just have to run it off."

"Oh, you're a runner." See? I knew it.

"Why does that depress you?" He laughs at my tone.

"I'm not depressed. I just hate running, and I always feel guilty about it." And before today, I was pretty sure I hated guys who went running regularly. At least one guy.

"So what do you do for exercise?" We're still playing the Get to Know You game.

"Panic."

He laughs, hard enough to startle people passing. But that wasn't funny. That was instinctive honesty.

"Okay. Moving on. What's your favorite color?" His laugh sounds like a person with asthma, wheezing. Why is that so cute?

"To look at, or to wear?"

"Is there a difference?"

29

"Absolutely. Blue to look at. Brown to wear."

"Brown? Really? Why?"

I shrug. "I like to blend in. Brown blends."

"Am I the first person to tell you that it's not working? You don't blend."

How do I answer that? Do I have to? I concentrate on keeping my legs moving forward while I process his comment. *You don't blend.* I don't even know what that means. I work very hard to ensure that I do, in fact, blend. What am I doing wrong?

He can tell I'm embarrassed. He moves on to the next question. "Who's your favorite musician?"

If I had any sense of cool, I'd probably be able to name someone who is topping charts and filling iPod playlists across the country and around the world. But I knew I couldn't carry the lie, so I don't try. "Paul Simon."

He looks pleased. I guess he's heard of him. "Really? Alone, or with Art?"

He knows Paul. And to know is to love. How perfect. "Either. Both. He's a master on the guitar." We've reached my apartment. I wonder if he'd come inside. Could I invite him in? Or is that something only a brazen hussy would do? Would he laugh at me? Or worse? Would he find a way to humiliate me for asking?

"Do you play?"

Do I play? Do I play what? I can feel the panic on my face.

He clarifies. "Is the guitar in your living room yours, or does one of your roommates play?"

"Oh, the guitar. Right. It's mine. I play a little."

"I'd love to hear you. Want to play for me?"

He's inviting himself in. Well, this is easy. Is this how it works for girls who are heroines?

30

"Sure. But I'm not great, so don't expect to be, you know, astounded or anything."

Climbing the stairs, I wonder if the apartment will be empty. I sure hope so. I'm not up for roommates right now. I have never read a romance novel peopled with characters like my roommates. They don't exactly inspire romance (at least not other people's). Good. Nobody's home.

I tell Ben to take a seat on the couch. "Want a drink?" I ask from the kitchen.

"Sure. What are you having?"

"Water. But you can have whatever you want, as long as it's in the fridge. We live on the honor system here, so if I need to borrow anything in the fridge, it's okay." I cringe; too much information again.

"Water's good," he says.

I come back to the living room and see Ben folded up on the couch, cradling my guitar. He's tuning, and he's got a good ear. Putting both glasses down on the side table, I ask the obvious. "You play?"

He looks at me funny. I can't tell what that look means. It almost seems like he's offended. No, too strong. Hurt. Oops. "We already talked about this, didn't we?" I guess. I have got to learn how to listen. He nods. "Sorry. Short-term memory loss. I was a little nervous earlier. About the study group and every-thing." *Everything related to you.* He starts to hand me the guitar, but I motion for him to keep it.

"You first," I tell him.

He plays "The Boxer"—a classic. He hums softly, and I hum the harmonies, so quietly he can't hear me. Which is just fine. He doesn't need to hear—it's fun simply to be humming along. I love the feeling of making music, any kind of music. After two songs he hands the guitar over to where I'm sitting on the floor. I play a couple of songs and watch his hands tapping on his knees. He seems really into the music. I guess he must have told me he loves music. I wish I could rewind the last few hours and find out what else he said. I don't want to make him have that hurt look again. I glance up at his face. He's grinning at me. My fingers freeze, and I forget how to play.

He stands up, and I know he's leaving. How long did I really expect him to stay, anyway? Well, I was hoping for longer than fifteen minutes. He's still smiling as he says, "Don't go anywhere, okay?" He heads for the door, and says, "Stay right there. Just a minute."

As soon as the door closes, I run to the window. I can see him jogging down the stairs. He stops at an ancient Subaru in the parking lot and pops the trunk. Pulling out a battered case, he starts running back up the stairs. I plop back onto the floor and try very hard to look like I've been sitting here, waiting, without any stalker tendencies like staring out windows and memorizing license plate numbers.

He knocks on the door. "Come in," I laugh. He pokes his head in.

"It's me," he says, as though maybe I was expecting someone else.

He returns to the couch and opens his case. Inside is a gorgeous honey-colored Gibson. I hear myself sigh. He pulls it out and tunes it quickly; I stare at that beautiful guitar. He sees me drooling.

"It's kind of an antique. Family heirloom. It's a 1942 J-45."

Do I know what that means? Do I care? I take a break from staring at the beautiful guitar to glance up at him again.

"It was my grandpa's, then my dad's. That's the end of the line, though. I'm never passing it on. It will be buried with me."

"It's fantastic," I whisper. There's a moan of longing in my voice that I hope he can't hear. It sounds a tiny bit like lust, and that's just embarrassing.

I listen as he begins another song. The tone is rich and full, and I can't imagine anything else adding points to this guy's hotness score. He starts singing, and after a few bars, I join in on the harmony again, this time a little louder. I watch him pick out some complicated patterns while I strum, and I let my eyes wander to his face. He's intense, bending over his guitar, watching his hands. When he glances over at me, his face lights right up. I can feel myself smiling, too.

"You're awesome," he says. "Choose another song."

I pick something easy so I can keep watching him. We start another song, and then another. When I finally glance over at the clock, it's 10:30.

"Sorry. I had no idea it was so late," I say, standing up on my sleeping legs. I lurch a little, but manage to get my guitar back on its stand.

"Oh. Is this late? Did you have somewhere you needed to be?" He looks embarrassed, as though he'd been keeping me from something.

"No, I just figured you had plans for tonight," I shrug, standing near the couch. This is what they call Giving Him an Out. I perfected this art after the humiliation of standing a little too close and holding on a little too tight. I am so past that now.

He smiles right at me again. My stomach does a lurch. "Nothing that can't wait."

What does that mean? That his girlfriend is the kind to wait around all night until he finishes playing songs on his guitar and finally decides to call her? Or that he really doesn't have anything else planned?

"So, are we done? Or do you want to hear one I wrote?" He wants to stay. He writes music, and he wants to stay.

"I'd love to hear it," I tell him. I'm still standing by the couch. If I stay here, I look impatient. If I go back to my spot on the floor, I can see him best, but my legs are sparking from sitting there for hours (hours!), so I climb onto the arm of the couch and sort of sit sideways to his arm. Hugging a pillow, I watch his hands. His song is simple, a repeated pattern with some strumming and some picking. I see him glance at my face, and I ask him if his song has words.

"Not yet. You should write some for me." He starts humming, the tune complementing the guitar accompaniment. When he's finished, I ask him to play it again. This time, I hum along, adding the harmony I hear in my head. From my new perch, I'm close enough for him to hear me.

"That's nice," he says. "You have a good voice."

I shrug. "Not really."

"Sure you do. We sound great together." He nudges my knee with his elbow. I steal another glance at the clock. I think he noticed, because he starts packing up his guitar.

I wish he wasn't leaving, but I know that eventually he has to get back to his life. "That was fun. Thanks." Thanks for walking me to study group. Thanks for telling me all sorts of things I didn't hear. Thanks for staying and playing and singing with me. Thanks for making me feel interesting.

"Yeah, it was fun. We'll have to do it again."

Absolutely. Any time. As he heads down the stairs, I realize that I have to get some chocolate in this apartment, and fast.

Next philosophy class, Dr. Younger has the day's goal projected from his laptop. Probably so nothing derails him too much.
By "nothing," of course I mean the girl on her existential journey.

Apparently we are going to practice clearly and completely
stating our personal views and then justify and defend them. I
have some personal views. Like the view from beneath as I walk
next to Ben, or the view from the auditorium chair as I stare at
the TA in art history. Or the view from my favorite booth at In
a Whirl where I can enjoy the adorable counter boy. There are
more, but they're not yet clearly and completely stated. *Oh, I am
a shallow idiot.*

I smile at my own ridiculous thoughts as I glance up.
Existential Journey Girl catches my eye and apparently thinks
I'm smiling at her. She slides into the seat next to me, says hi,
and opens her bag. If I didn't know better, I'd probably still
think she was a normal person. She's acting normal now. She
even used a normal voice. But don't worry. I've already determined to hate her. Because I know her. I knew girls (at least one
in particular) just like this. She's a pretender. So I'll pretend too.
I'll pretend she's not here.

Deciding to look busy, I compose an e-mail to my mom.
I ask her to send some sheet music I left at home. I don't send
her e-mail as often as I should, but it's just a formality anyway.
She certainly doesn't miss me. She's experiencing such a burst
of freedom with me gone, even beyond taking strange vacations.
It's only been a couple of weeks, but she's already used bizarre
words like "Pilates class" and "girls' night out" and "the Gourmet
Diners' Guild." Even if I had a car here, I can't see me driving

six hours home only to find a note taped to the fridge, telling me that she's gone to a scuba lesson.

So I type my note, like a good daughter, but my act of distraction isn't working. The girl isn't ignoring me like I'm ignoring her. She's leaning over, way inside my personal space.

"What are you doing? You can't be taking notes yet. Class hasn't even started," she says, as though maybe I haven't noticed. She's still using her normal voice, not the airy one. If she leans any closer, she's going to topple onto my shoulder.

I shrug. Determined to be vague, I keep my eyes on my screen. She keeps talking. After her "I like your computer" comment and her "I'm never this early to class" comment and her "Don't you love these lectures" comment, I'm sure she must be getting some sense of a hint. Has she noticed that, aside from a polite nod and maybe a *hmm* noise, I'm not actually responding to her?

Maybe she really can't tell. Maybe she's one of those people who everyone (except me) likes. Maybe she's never had anyone ignore her before. Maybe she's used to people listening to her. Maybe she doesn't care what I think. Maybe she just likes the sound of her own voice. Maybe I shouldn't be worried about it, because maybe I don't care that much.

I've learned not to care about a lot of things over the past few years. I'm telling you, once you learn this skill, it's pretty easy to slip it into different life experiences. For instance, once you learn not to care that a certain someone named for a famous American outlaw has caused you to be humiliated in front of dozens of people, you can easily not care that you left the apartment with no makeup on, or that your zipper is down, or that you're wearing smoothie on your shirt. Liberating, that's what it is.

# Chapter Four

I've just finished studying for the afternoon and I turn my phone back on.

Chirp. There's a text. It's from *him*. I wonder if he really has nothing better to do than give me attention I don't deserve. I shouldn't complain, really, because someday I'm going to have to go back to being Sarah the Invisible, closet reader of other people's fantasy lives.

BUSY? WNT TO WAK?

What is *wak?* Sometimes I hate texts.

I respond, NEED ICE CREAM FIRST.

I wait a minute to give him time to remember that there are dozens, if not hundreds, of girls lined up to go *wak* with him, whatever that is—oh, right, *walk*—and maybe none of them will demand ice cream. This is a perfect out for him. He can tell me to get my ice cream by myself and then he'll disappear.

But he doesn't.

2:00. ICE CREAM FRST. THEN WE WAK.

It's ten minutes till. Trying to tame my idiotic hair, I pull it back with an elastic. Those girls with smooth, shiny sheets of hair have no idea how good they have it. I dig in my closet to unearth some shoes. When he says we're going for a walk, what does he have in mind? Are we hiking the side of a cliff? Probably not. We're pretty short on cliffs here. But he doesn't seem like the wander-through-town-looking-at-shops kind of guy either. I know there are some runner-type shoes in here somewhere. I'm sure I haven't worn them in the few weeks since I moved into the apartment, but nobody who lives with me is going to be stealing my shoes. They're not that great. (The shoes, I mean.)

I dig them out. They are sort of smashed, and they look like they've been sat on for a couple of months, but I wiggle them on. As I stand up to go find a water bottle, I catch my reflection in the mirror. My shoulders sag a little at the sight of me. My T-shirt says "Keep It Reel" with a graphic of a roll of movie film, and these yoga sweats do nothing to hide the fact that I'm a girl with hips. *Oh, well. That Reubens painter would have loved me.*

The thought crosses my mind that Chel would be so proud of me if I bothered to put on some real clothes. Then the doorbell rings and I know it's too late.

"Hey, Sarah. Caramel Pecan or Peanut Butter Cup?" He's holding out two massive waffle cones.

"Shoot. That was nice of you, but I'm allergic to nuts," I tell him. "If I eat either one of those, my throat will close up in seconds. I will stop breathing and turn blue and pass out. Then my body will go into shock and I may have seizures. It's probably not something you want to see."

His face falls. "Oh, I'm so sorry. I just wanted to surprise you. Sorry. Look, let's toss these, and you can order whatever you want. Sorry, that was dumb."

He just said "sorry" three times. *Three.* Time to end the madness.

"Okay, I was just kidding. I'm not allergic to anything. I want the caramel one."

He looks down at me, a confused and annoyed look on his face. I can tell he's faking it, though. Sure enough, he bursts out laughing again. (Note to self: Remember to keep saying stupid things. The laugh is so worth him thinking you're an idiot.)

"Come on. Let's walk while we eat," he says. "That way, if you have any reactions to your ice cream, I can just walk away and leave you twitching. No one will ever know I was involved."

As if he were involved. I wish.

We walk through my neighborhood, out into blocks of houses that all look pretty much the same behind their fences and yards. Ben talks while I lick my cone, the sugar rush combining with some serious adrenaline just from being near him. I wonder if he has any idea what power he has here. Does he know that medically, he's causing some havoc with me? My heart rate is probably doubled. My nerves are zinging. Even my nose is on high alert—I can smell the dusty decay of autumn leaves in the sun. Wow. That was some great line. I must have read it somewhere—like in a cheap paperback borrowed from the back of the library.

This moment could be from a romance novel. Except there's no heavy breathing. And I'm not wearing a corset. And Ben isn't a pirate or a prince in disguise or a wealthy European land-owner or a dashing older gentleman with a crazy wife locked in a tower. And I am not a romance-novel kind of character. Not even close.

"What have you got going on tonight?"

I wish I could make up something spectacular, but

believable. Like that I have steeplechase practice or that I need to wallpaper my grandmother's living room. But I don't even lie.

"Nothing. Homework is done, and I'm plan-free."

"Want to watch a movie?" he asks so casually that I know he's just being nice.

"Sure," I say. Now he can tell me to go ahead and watch one, he won't stop me. Ha, ha. Like I haven't heard that before. *Go ahead, pretty boy. Give it your best shot.* The thought comes unbidden. But he's not like that. He's not an outlaw. He's a gentleman.

"I'm taking care of my sister's apartment for a few days, so if you want, we could go over there and maybe get a pizza and you could help me with my paper that's due tomorrow and then we could watch a movie."

"I love how you slipped that part about me doing your homework in there," I say. But I do love that part. It means he's serious. He wants me around. Do I care so much that the reason is to do his homework? I guess not.

He laughs. "It's almost done. But I could use some proof-reading help. If you don't mind."

If I don't mind? He doesn't just want my company—he wants my brain, too. Well, that's perfectly fine with me. He can use my brain, because I don't need it for any of the staring I plan to do. Just like my mom tells me, there are a lot of qualities more important and lasting than beauty, and I have them in abundance. I'm sure there was a compliment in there somewhere. Thanks, Mom.

We walk to his sister's apartment. It's in the basement of the sweetest little house, complete with a flower-lined, brick walkway. We go down the staircase behind the house to the apartment door that's painted bright red. I decide not to tell him that I've always wanted a house with a red door. It's a relief to recognize that I've finally kept a piece of information to myself.

The apartment is beautiful—brighter than I expect for a basement. There's matching furniture here, and pictures on the walls. I stare at the gorgeous couple in one photo.

"That's my sister Megan and her fiancé, Will," Ben tells me.

They're a beautiful sight, and I can imagine a perfect romance novel starring them: *They grew up together, but were kept apart by the demands of his snobby family, forced to endure years of forbidden letters and secret contact. Finally his family was won over by her charm and beauty and gave their consent to the match. Now they plan a lavish wedding followed by an escape to a tropical island hideaway where mystery and adventure await them.*

I need a new hobby.

Ben's paper is in pretty good shape. He's a decent writer—his statements are clear, and he has good transitions, but his spelling is atrocious.

"Do you actually know how to use a spell-check?" I must know.

"You mean all those red squiggles on my screen? I like them. They're so pretty." He laughs softly, like he really doesn't mind that I'm marking up his paper. "No, I turn my monitor off when I write. Then I don't get distracted by my own mistakes. It's a little trick I've learned."

"Well, that's one way to do it." I shrug. I read a few more sentences, but I can feel him watching, and it makes me nervous. I glance up at him again.

He's looking at me with his head down, but his eyes up. Is that what "hooded eyes" means? It's totally hot in here. Are there functional windows in this basement?

My face turns red as I stare at the paper. I look over at him again, and he's smiling at me.

He is totally distracting. I focus on the paper, offer a few suggestions, and circle all his misspelled words. This part takes a while.

Looking up, I see he's still watching me. "Don't worry. I'm not thrashing it. You don't have much more to do."

He shrugs, like an apology. "Yeah, sorry about the spelling thing. Letters just don't like to stay in order for me."

I'm not sure gravity is staying in order for me right now. I need a deep breath and maybe a dramatic face-slap to get me back on track here. "Once you fix that, though, you're pretty much there. Just give me a couple more minutes."

"I didn't want to stop your hard work. Thanks for helping me fix it. So what do you like on your pizza?"

I'm willing to ride this out. When the movie's over and the lights come on, he's bound to discover that his arm is around my shoulders. And that his fingers are touching the back of my neck so lightly I wasn't sure until right now that they were there. When the lights are on, he'll let go of that crazy, out-of-control curl that he seems to be wrapping around his pinky. I have the strangest feeling in my stomach. It's roller-coaster-y, but I'm sitting perfectly still. So still, in fact, that my body is permanently taking on the contours of the couch. I'm sure I have muscles that are locked around the shape of every seam in this cushion.

I don't want to move because I don't want him to remember who is sitting here inside the curve of his arm. I don't want him to come to his senses before it's absolutely necessary. If

I'm honest with myself I can admit that since I expect this will never happen again, I want to enjoy every second.

But enjoyment is not what I'm experiencing here. Definitely more like dread. I dread the moment the light has to come on. I fear the discomfort the next time he has to look at my face. I'll be mortified that he has seen me in all my ponytail-and-sweats glory. He seems gallant enough that he'll be embarrassed for . . . for what? For giving too much attention to a girl who doesn't deserve it. For forgetting himself and thinking I was someone else. Anyone else.

I want to look at his face, but I would rather perform invasive surgery on myself than turn my head toward Ben right now. So I imagine what he looks like as he stares at the screen. (What movie are we watching? I have no idea what's going on.) His hair must be nearly touching his eyebrows. Those eyebrows. They are the perfect shape to accent his eyes. I love how his eyes go wide with surprise and then crinkle up when he laughs at something I say.

Does his face do that for everyone? Or is he only surprised to be amused by me?

I have always had a thing for good teeth, and I thought "good" meant straight, white, and even—teeth that glint in the sunlight—but I find myself staring at Ben's teeth (not right now, certainly), and I love how his front tooth sits just a bit forward from the rest. It gives his smile character. I'm all over character.

"You were pretty into that film," Ben says as he stretches his arms over his head.

"Yeah, I've never seen it." Not before, and not tonight. Now that it's over, I have every reason to turn and face him. No matter how this ends, I can at least stare at his great face for a few unembarrassed minutes now.

My two o'clock break can't come soon enough on Thursday. Not that I have anything really meaningful to tell my fellow proofreaders, but I want to shake off the jitters. As we start walking toward the vending machine, Shari stuns us all.

"I had the greatest date this week," she says, her voice full of confidence and even a little laugh. Not what I'd expect to hear from our resident nerd.

"Right on." Tandy is the first to recover from the surprise. "What did you do?"

"Pizza and a movie." Shari shrugs, as if it's totally natural to call pizza and a movie with a guy a date.

*Wait. Is it?*

*Maybe for Shari, but not for me.*

*But what if Ben thought it was a date?*

*Then he would have asked someone else, wouldn't he?*

*Oh, right.*

But I want a male opinion on this. Dean?

"Hey, where's Dean?" I ask. The other girls look behind us. He's not there.

"Bio break," Maura says, nodding.

We look at her, clearly not getting it.

"Biology? Physiology? He's probably in the bathroom. You know—bio break."

Tandy bursts out laughing. But then she catches herself, and her eyes widen with the look I'm starting to recognize as her Conspiracy Theory Face. "No, wait. Maybe he stayed behind in the cube. Maybe he has a private meeting with the Boss."

"Eww," Maura groans, and Shari wrinkles her nose.

"No, come on. Why not? He's cute, and she's lonely. It's perfect. He worked here all summer, remember? Maybe they got together . . ." Her voice trails off, and I know she's trying to compose the unlikely scene in her head. She obviously doesn't have much practice in this.

I interrupt her lame attempt at creating a romance novel. "Do you actually think that Dean is having an affair with the Boss?"

"You make it sound so tawdry," Tandy complains. "Of course I don't think that. I don't believe half of what I say." She smiles and slips a dollar into the vending machine. "Anyone want half a Twix?"

I pass, but recognize that my chance to ask them to define my weekend outing has passed, too. I still don't know if what I had was a date, or a study session, or a purely platonic hang-out. But looking back, I can admit that it was mostly fun.

Maura and Shari split the other half of Tandy's chocolate bar, and we head back to the cubicle a minute early, Tandy looking to uncover some tabloid news. No such luck. Dean is leaning back in his chair, talking into his cell.

"Okay. Thanks, Mom. See you." Pause. "Yeah. Love you, too."

Aw. Sweet.

# Chapter Five

I'm sprawled on the empty living room floor working on my homework for Monday, when Lauren crashes through the front door. She looks flustered, and she's certainly in a hurry.

"Hi," I try, even though there is nearly no chance she'll respond.

She makes actual eye contact and nods before she tears down the hall to her bedroom. For a second I wonder what she's rushing to, then I figure maybe I don't want to know. Maybe she's just hurrying away—away from me and the need to make polite conversation. Wait, she's never felt that need. Honestly, the girl just doesn't talk.

I wonder again how I ended up here. Not just at this university, a half day's drive from home. That's pretty obvious. Chel brought me here with some e-mailed photos of the TA. And a decent scholarship helped. But how did this whole apartment thing come about? Maybe I was too lazy to find anything better. It seemed good enough at the time. Even though I don't know the other girls and the couches are ugly and the kitchen table only seats three, at least I have my own room.

But it would be nice to have a friend in the building.

*But what if the friend turned out to be like the girls in high school?*

*Be fair. Not all the girls in high school were evil.*

*Okay, not all. Not Chel. But most of them would have loved nothing more than to have a chance to see someone looking like an idiot.*

*And then talk about it. Forever.*

*Just be glad Chel's around. She's enough. She stood by me before, in the face of the spiteful, gossiping harpies.*

*Yeah, until she moved away to school and left me swimming with the sharks.*

*That was not personal. It was a good opportunity for her and you know it.*

*Yeah, I guess. But lonely, right?*

*Well, at least I know I'll always have the other half of my brain.*

*Right. The clever half.*

*Or the crazy half.*

*You know you love me.*

There's no use pretending that I'm some fashionably waiflike girl who doesn't eat anything but celery and bean sprouts, so when Ben asks if I want to get another cone with him, I get all shivery with anticipation. For the ice cream, too.

"Tell me a story," he commands from behind his coconut

crème chip waffle cone. "Not anything related to art history. My brain is full."

Our study group was pretty intense tonight.

I hesitate, pretending to think up a great one for him, but really, my mouth is very full of black cherry chocolate. I look skyward and let the sweetness slide down.

"Okay. There's this girl. She looks normal enough. I think she's actually pretty cute. But here's the thing. Something's not connected in her brain. She's a little strange. Different from most people in the class. And from all the normal people I've ever seen. Okay, she's completely nuts."

I pause for a bite. Ben's eyes are laughing with me.

"She has mistaken philosophy class for her own personal psychoanalytical session. Freud would love her. She's a dreamer. Every week she has a new dream to share. As though it has something to do with learning to formulate arguments."

"Is that what you do in philosophy? Argue?" He looks intrigued, and a little horrified. Like he would hate that.

"Yeah, plus a little shouting and throwing some chairs. It's pretty out of control. No. We talk about logic. Anyway—about Dream Girl. Today she walked into class, sat in her chair, and shut her eyes. She had her palms down on her desk like she was feeling for pre-earthquake compression waves or something."

Ben laughs again. I love to hear that. I'm not even sure this would be funny to anyone who hadn't been in the class. But he's laughing with me, so I don't care.

"She was deep breathing through her nose and pretty much making herself as conspicuous as possible. Class starts, lecture gets underway, and she raises her hand. Eyes still closed. So I looked up and saw poor old Dr. Younger take a bracing breath. He actually closed his own eyes for a tiny second. Maybe he was hoping to find some of her serenity. I would have just ignored her. But maybe he was afraid she could see through her closed eyes. I guess he couldn't avoid calling on her—or maybe he's just a glutton for punishment—but he gave her permission to speak. She opened her eyes and informed us that in her latest dream in the Unseen Dimension, her eyes were placed behind her ears on her head. I wish I could have seen that. Apparently the Universe was letting her know she ought to listen before she looks."

"What did the professor say?"

I don't know why Ben finds this interesting, but I'll keep talking as long as he sits across the table. I mean, he asked.

"He thanked her for sharing and moved on, kind of sweeping her out of the way. She's crazy enough not to have noticed. If she didn't bug me so much, I'd like to pick her brain for an hour. I'd love to figure out what is misfiring. I know there's a mind in there somewhere. And she's capable of talking normally. I've heard her. She's working hard to keep something hidden, because, you know, she's that kind of girl—playing all innocent and sweet. It's totally annoying. And I can't figure it out. Who is the act supposed to be for? Is she rehearsing for some part in a movie? Does she really think it's a good personality type to develop? I'm not seeing it."

I know I sound snarky, but I'm right. She is the most annoying person I've seen since I've been here. And I've seen a bunch of annoying people.

Ice cream is gone. Too bad. Now there's not a real reason for us to stay here.

"Thanks for the treat," I tell him. I'm being polite now. Helping him excuse himself now that the business of eating is over.

"Do you have much homework?" he asks.

I tell him about two papers due Monday.

"Want to go to the library and work on them?"

Does he mean with him?

I shrug. "I think I have all my research done. I'll just finish up the writing part at home."

"Okay. So I'll see you Monday for class?"

Why does he keep acting so nice? Doesn't he have other friends he'd rather hang out with? Wait, why do I care? This is fun, being friends with him. And I'm being careful not to put myself in any place where he could pull a Jesse James—make me feel comfortable, then whip out the gun.

# Chapter Six

I t's such a perfect day. I don't want to be inside, so I'm flopped on the raggedy patch of grass outside my apartment building. My philosophy paper is finished, and very nearly brilliant. I've dissected a few statements from the president's last address to the nation and clearly stated my own opposing views.

Now I just have to finish this character assassination for literature. Daisy Buchanan is going down. Now there's a girl straight out of a romance novel. All breathy and passive-aggressive, turning people's lives upside down just because she can. My two brains start arguing again.

*Don't be too hard on her. You would be her if you thought you could get away with it.*

*Never. She has no principles.*

*Yeah, maybe not. But men fall at her feet.*

*There's more to life than—you know what? I'm not really interested in finishing that sentence anymore.*

*Probably a good idea.*

My internal discussion is interrupted by the appearance of

Ben—here at my scrubby lawn square. He's carrying his Gibson and wearing a Yankees ball cap. I peck furiously at my keyboard so I look like I'm working, rather than talking to myself.

"Hey, what's the point of owning a cell phone if you don't take it with you when you leave the house?" He offers me that smile where his tooth barely pokes out from his lips.

I can feel splotches of red coloring my neck. I gracelessly shift from lying on my stomach to sitting on the lawn, brushing dead grass clippings from my shirt and elbows.

"I'm trying to concentrate here. I just have to finish sacrificing Daisy on the altar of stupid women." I can tell I've lost him.

I try to clarify. "You know, Daisy Buchanan?" No reply. "Gatsby? Fitzgerald?" He looks like he's never heard any of these words before, so I back up. "Okay, I have to write a paper about a character whose motivations I disapprove of. So I picked Daisy Buchanan. She's from *The Great Gatsby,* which my literature professor assigned us read. That would be my fourth time. And I hate her more every time I read about her. So she's being deconstructed, or something." I wave to my laptop, as if maybe it was taking Daisy down for me.

"Why do you hate her?"

Could he possibly be interested?

"I could give you a list of very good reasons, all of which you would agree with. But mainly I think I hate her because she makes men miserable, and I could never do that."

"Yeah, you're way too nice for that," he says, smiling that smile that makes me lose focus.

"No, you misunderstand me. I totally would if I were capable. I'm just not built with the options that make guys fall at my feet. I can't do the quiet, breathy voice that makes people lean closer just to hear whatever magical thing I'm about to say."

"You mean like that girl in your philosophy class?" He does a little pant-pant-giggle with a totally exaggerated eyelash flutter.

I laugh, and realize that yes, that's exactly what I mean.

"Yeah, like that. I can't pretend not to care about anything just to make me seem all modern and unconcerned. You can read it, if you want." I turn my laptop toward him, but he waves it off.

"I think it's better if you just tell me. If I read your paper, I probably wouldn't get it anyway. You know," he hurries on, "because I've never read the book."

"It's a great book. And it's short. You should try it sometime."

He gives me a strange face again, that adorable confused look. I hit save and snap my computer shut.

"So what brings you here?" I ask him.

"I need a break. I've been writing papers, too, you know. Not papers that make me angry enough to kill pretend people—just papers. So I think we should go to the park and make music for the migrating birds, or something."

"That was so poetic. Let me put this away and I'll grab my guitar." I jump up from the ground, then lean back down to pick up my laptop, and crash into Ben's forehead. Apparently he was bending over to hand me the computer, and I wasn't watching.

*Is that possible? Aren't we always watching?*

*Ouch.*

⌒

"How do you feel about weddings?" Ben asks while we sit on a wooden bench rubbed smooth from years of birdwatchers and playground moms.

"I'm in favor of them, but let's not rush into anything." Did I really just say that?

Luckily he laughs. I love hearing his laugh, seeing that one tooth pushing out a little from the others. I pick out a complicated little pattern on my guitar I've been trying to perfect.

"My sister Megan is getting married next week. We went to her apartment, remember?"

*Remember? Oh, was that with you? Yeah, I guess I remember.*

"There's a party after at our house. Food, music, way too many relatives—you know. D'you want to come?"

"Sure." The word leaps out of my mouth before I even have time to think about it. Before I can assess the situation. Why does he want me to come? Will I have to wear a dress? Will I sit, stand, and wander with Ben? Or should I bring a friend to entertain me while he works the room? Why did I say yes? I don't even know his sister. Do I want to know her? And does it even matter? She's not going to remember one extra guest at her wedding reception.

Do I care more about the unknown parts of this adventure that are freaking me out? Or more about the fact that Ben has, yet again, invited me to be with him?

"Chel, I have a very urgent request for your services. Call me instantly," I bark into her voice mail.

She calls back, but it takes her forever. Seventeen minutes! Where are the manners, people?

"Hey, what's up?" she says.

How can she be so calm? Has she no idea that we are now living in a state of emergency?

"I have to go to a wedding reception with Ben. And all his family. And also me. In the same room or something. Help me." Oh, that whiny voice. No leading lady would ever whine. Another reason I'm no leading lady. Add it to the list.

"Okay, honey? I'm at work right now."

Oh, yeah. Oops.

"I will come over when I'm done, and we will get you all calmed down. Now here is what you need to do right now. Take a deep breath." She waits. "I can't hear you," she sings.

I breathe audibly.

"Better. Okay. Now you need some ice cream. Not the whole carton. Just three bites. Go. I'll wait."

I walk to the freezer and pull out a pint. My breathing calms down as my mouth is coated in beautiful butterfat.

"Okay," I manage through a mouthful. "Got it."

"Now sit down and read a book for a few minutes. I'm off work at two, and I'll be there. Okay? Will you be fine until then?"

She's such a good friend. "Yeah, I'm good. Thanks, Chel."

"See you soon, sweetie. It's going to be all right. Everything's fine. Just fine." She's murmuring to me like the words are a lullaby.

"Okay. See you soon. Thank you," I whisper. Even my voice is calmer. She's a miracle worker.

I snap my phone shut and the spell is broken. My heart is thrashing around again, and it would probably leap right out of my neck if my throat weren't threatening to close up completely. I know I can't call Chel at work again, so I opt for the next best treatment. Clutching the ice cream pint, I head for my bed.

Chel finds me huddled under my covers with the empty pint of peach ice cream still clutched in my hand. She will never know about the empties under the bed (toffee and cookie dough).

"Okay. To business. Get out of bed. Nothing traumatic has happened to you. You have received an invitation to a party. You are not dying, or even ill. Get up. Seriously." She rips the covers back. I flinch like she's torn a Band-Aid off the inside of my elbow.

She gives me a slightly disgusted look as she peels my fingers off the ice cream container.

*Please don't look under the bed*, I pray.

"Good. Now. Who is getting married?" She is so efficient it's almost scary.

"Ben's sister Megan."

"Megan of the apartment where you didn't watch the movie?"

I nod.

"Is the reception inside or outside?"

I shrug.

"Will the wedding ceremony happen at the same time, or before?"

I shake my head. I don't know.

She gives me a look reminding me that I am pathetic, but she loves me anyway. "No problem. We will work on your clothes, and the rest will follow. As it always does."

Walking to my closet, Chel looks confident and hopeful. Then she opens the door. Her spine wrinkles in defeat. I see her take a deep breath and plunge in, sliding hangers and peering into the dark corners.

"Didn't you bring any dresses with you to college?" What she doesn't add is *you idiot*. I love her for that.

"I know there are a couple of skirts back there. You know,

in case I have to go to the symphony or a funeral or something while I'm here."

She doesn't seem to think I'm funny.

"Budget?" she asks.

Blank stare.

"What's in your bank account?"

"Why?" I am lost again.

"This is an emergency. We shop. No arguing. Do you want my help or not?"

Well, duh. "I want your help. There's money in the account. Go get me something great."

"Oh, no. No, no—you're coming. And trying. And experimenting, and—according to my plan—succeeding. Let's go. But first, wash your face. You're wearing way more than just the peach ice cream there, sister."

# Chapter Seven

The mall is a place of mystery and mazes. It contains a terrifying amount of information that I can't process. Or won't process, or something. It freaks me out by its size, its variety, and its chaos. I've managed to go all these years without being the kind of girl who hangs out in a mall. I'm a pro at ordering clothes online—just what I need, and already know I like. I find what fits and can get it in three colors so there are no worries about being seen in the same thing over and over. Not that I really care.

But Chel thinks I should. And Chel cares. She's very good at all things clothes, and so, by default, she's good at the mall. There are stores just for fingernails in this place. Just for jewelry. Just for cheap neckties. Just for chocolate (a point of interest I've never put too much thought into before—shame on me). Just for little girls who want to dress like ceramic dolls. Just for little girls who want to dress like teenagers. Just for older women who want to dress like teenagers. And apparently just for teenagers who want to dress like older women, or so I've heard.

But there's also food. And I'm not talking about the store

dedicated to every kind of protein powder mix-in available. No, I mean the good stuff. White, hot, buttered starch. Pretzels, breadsticks, and popcorn—oh, my.

I've just about got myself pumped up for this outing and I'm ready to jump off the bus at the mall with Chel, when she pulls me back down in the seat.

"We're not getting out here."

"But this is the mall," I say slowly, as if to a person who wasn't raised in a mall.

She takes my hand and shakes her head. "Yes. I know. Thank you. Please sit down. We'll take the next one."

So at the next stop, I get up and follow Chel out the door. Upon hitting the sidewalk, I know I am way out of my world. Chel guides me up the block and we pass very attractive people moving from here to there. I watch my shoes. I can hear Chel saying hi to beautiful strangers as if such interaction were normal. She stops in front of a window full of mannequins that I can only describe as *chic*. I glance at Chel with her accessories and her confidence and her groovy haircut and realize that I am now in her zone: the Chel Zone.

The store—excuse me—the *boutique* is called Fiori Bianchi, and I know instinctively that I will never be able to (1) fit into, (2) afford, or (3) appear in public wearing anything from this place. I look into Chel's eyes and prepare to tell her that we're going to have to catch the next bus back to the mall. She smiles that smile people save for lost kittens, newborn babies, and the very old: *You poor, sweet, helpless thing. Let me just stroke your head.*

"Okay, here's the plan." She has a vise grip on my arm so I can't bolt. "You will not buy anything here. You cannot afford it. I cannot afford it. But the women working here will never know that. We will enter with confidence. We will not waste time browsing, because I know you will choose a brown dress, which will never do. So we will do this my way, and you will smile. Like you mean it. Start now."

I wince under her clutch.

"That isn't a smile."

"Please loosen up on the arm," I say with a plastic grin.

"Mmm. Better. Sorry about the welts," she says, and she opens the door.

Instead of a laser-sensor beep or even an antique bell over the door, there is a set of wooden wind chimes to announce us. Chel puts her hand to my back and marches me forward. Only someone standing behind us would see that her finger and thumb are on either side of my spine, ready to pinch and control me into submission. That won't be necessary. I've decided to submit. I'm even smiling. Mostly.

"Hi, ladies. I hope you can help us. My friend needs a great outfit to wear to an outdoor wedding reception next weekend. Any ideas?" Chel's voice is powerful, confident, and just loud enough for the women standing in front of us to hear. No other heads turn, and nobody else even seems to notice that we're there. Not that there's a crowd in here. It looks like I'm getting personalized service whether I want it or not.

The smiles on these women's faces are a whole lot more sincere than mine. They start touching me. One grabs my hand and looks at my skin, first on the palm, then on the back. Then she stares into my face. I forget to smile.

The other woman, tall and olive-skinned, stands to the side of me. She pushes my hair off my neck and then pulls my T-shirt into a bunch at my back.

*What is she doing to me?*

*Checking out your figure. Or lack thereof.*
*I don't want anyone checking out this figure.*
*Then say something, dummy.*

"Um, hi. What are you doing?" I have on my most polite voice, but somehow terror is still written all over me.

"Don't worry. This is simply a preliminary look." She sounds like Sophia Loren. "If you let me take a look, I'll spare you the trouble of trying on a lot of things that won't suit you."

I wonder if the shop owners had to advertise for a beautiful Italian woman to work here—you know, for atmosphere. But whether or not she's a plant, she seems confident and capable. And her accent is convincing. I try to stand still and hold in my abs.

Chel has the look of the huntress in her eyes. Dropping my arm, she follows her radar straight to a display of these classy little dresses. *Little* is the key word. They look like long tank tops. Or short slips. Sort of Roaring Twenties for girls with shoulders, but no hips or rear ends. I know I sort of agreed to work this shopping trip Chel's way, but I have to put a stop to this before anything too humiliating happens.

"No. Not a chance," I say, loud enough for Chel and the women groping me to hear. Turning, Chel doesn't even try to hide her look of clothing nirvana. Then all three of them speak at once.

"It's not for *you*," Chel snorts.

"No. Those are not made for this kind of figure." The Italian woman says it as though I actually have a figure, and I'd like to laugh.

"We'll find you something perfect. Don't worry." This from the woman who is holding my face, tipping my chin up and down, left and right.

Apparently I am the only person here who has no idea what she's doing.

The accent lady asks, "Generally a four? A six?"

I feel like she's speaking some language I don't recognize. My blank stare answers for me.

"What size are you, Sarah? Four or six?" Chel clarifies, sending a pitying look to the women who are forced to dress the idiot.

"Um, six on a good day. More like eight, I guess."

The Italian lady drops my shirt and puts her hands directly on my waist, pressing between my ribs and hips. "Oh, no. Not in the right dress." She smiles into my eyes, and I decide that if she can make me a size four, I won't hate her or her maybe-fake accent ever again.

She leads me to a brocaded armchair near a three-way mirror, and I catch a glimpse of me in my jeans and scruffy shoes. These poor women must be running to their caffeine stashes behind the counter to ramp up for the job ahead. But as they return, they don't look grouchy, or even resigned. They look excited. And their arms are already full.

"I need to have full shoulder coverage," I tell them. Better to lay it out on the line right away.

Chel rolls her eyes.

"And also nothing too short. Or tight. Or, you know, plunging. Or shiny. I don't want to look so . . . obvious."

Without even a visible sigh, the woman with the accent picks two dresses out of her pile and hangs them on a rail behind her. One looks like it is made out of a handkerchief and some ribbons. The other is gold. Like Egyptian-goddess gold. I manage to smile my thanks that those went straight to the rejection rack.

"Sarah, is it?" The Italian lady smiles. "I'm Luciana. If you need any different sizes right away, I'll be over here finding you some shoes and a bag so you can see the total ensemble."

And just like that they open a door and push me inside a huge dressing room with fabric-covered walls and a lighted mirror. All those dresses are lined up on a rail, hanging in a neat row. I believe that some people would find this pleasant. Luxurious. I'm going more with dreadful.

Even though I'm alone, I feel shy to grab tags and read the prices. I glance out of the corner of my eye, but there are no visible numbers. The tags have been tucked away, better to avoid vulgar displays like dollar amounts. I actually look around the dressing room as though someone could be watching, then sneak a tag out from inside a sleeve.

Audible intake of breath. *Three hundred and sixty-eight dollars?*

*What are we doing in this store?*

For once, my minds are in agreement. It's very creepy.

*Okay. Here's the deal. Chel made it very clear that we're not buying here. Just experimenting. So no more looking at prices. They are the least of our worries. There are much scarier things going on in this place.*

*Oh, come on. What are you afraid of?*

*What if I put on one of these dresses and look like a slob?*

*You mean as opposed to the way you look right now?*

*Not helping.*

*Just go. This is supposed to be fun, you know.*

*Yeah, so I've heard.*

I pull off my shoes, jeans, and T-shirt. Already something is different. Not that I go trying on clothes all that often, but I can tell that this lighting does a whole lot more for me than the discount department store's standard flickering neon. I'm not interested in going into too many details, here, but let's just say that there were no visible dimples where dimples should not be.

Methodically starting at the left and working my way across the bar, I preview each dress that Luciana and her colleague have selected for me. I'm planning to bust through them all in a row when I see the most fabulous dress of all time. If ice had a color, this would be it. It's so perfectly light blue with a little gray and maybe the tiniest hint of silver, but totally not bling-bling. With the conviction that this is the dress that I was born to wear, I unzip, slip it off the hanger, and start to pull it over my hips.

"Baggage," I curse.

Chel is standing guard at the door. "What's wrong?"

"This dress, the dress that was made for me, my destined very perfect clothing, won't go over my tush," I whine.

"Try pulling it on over your head."

Oh. Well, that's different. Wow. It settles in fairly perfect splendor over my shoulders, sliding in at the waist.

"Chel? Zip me up?"

She walks in, eying me objectively. She doesn't even gasp in wonder at the stunning dazzlement I'm wearing. She just does up my zipper and stands back.

"Come out and look in the big mirror," she commands.

I feel awesome. Who knew that all it would take to instill self-esteem is a totally overpriced dress?

"Good, right?" I know it's fabulous, but I still need feedback.

"Good cut. Good fabric. Wrong color, though. Next."

I stare at her in disbelief. Is she serious? I have never looked this excellent in my life. I am on the verge of something here, I can feel it. And she says "next"?

"What? What are you looking at?" she says. My inefficient standing and staring seem to be annoying Chel. Maybe as annoying as her *totally not noticing my hotness!*

"But, this dress. It's perfect. And . . . well, look at me. I look . . ." I break off, wondering if I'm overstepping decorum to proclaim my own beauty.

"You definitely have the right body for a dress like this. But look at your face. You have big purple raccoon eyes. The color doesn't work for you. Try something else."

"But, Chel, I'm in love with this color. It's the most beautiful fabric I've ever seen." There's no hiding the whining now. I want her to take it all back. The raccoon comment. The *next*. The lack of validation. I give her the patented what-kind-of-friend-are-you-anyway look and she rolls her eyes.

"You can get a bedspread made out of this fabric as long as you never let anyone see you in bed. That's all I'm saying. Go try the next one."

I go. I try. And I try. And I put on dresses that I would never have chosen. And, what do you know? Some of them look even better than the Ice-Blue Dress of Destiny. Standing in front of the mirror in an orange floral with a swingy shawl thing over my shoulders, I tell Chel, "Look. And tell me the truth. Is this the world's greatest magic mirror, or do I really look like that?"

She stands beside me and we look at our reflections. She looks the same as ever—fantastic. "This is really you," she says, squeezing my shoulder.

"But," my breath catches in my throat for a second, "but I don't look fat." Wonder colors my voice for once rather than a whine.

Luciana hears me, takes a sliding step toward us, and smiles into the mirror over my other shoulder. "Certainly not. Feminine, yes. Bordering on voluptuous. But definitely feminine."

*She's right,* I realize with surprise. *Would you look at that? There's no hiding the hips, though.*

*Apparently I don't need to hide them. They can sit here under this waist. This hourglass-y, smaller-than-we-thought waist.*

*Yeah, okay. Looks good. Go, you.*

*Why, thank you. Let's go try on another great dress.*

Here are some things I learned on this expedition with Chel:

1. Putting on fantastic shoes makes a good dress a great dress.

2. I can get away with more than I thought, fashionwise.

3. Maybe shopping with a friend is not completely painful.

4. "The Little Black Dress" is not a myth. It is true and it exists.

5. If it won't pull up from the floor, it might pull down from the top. If at first you don't succeed and all that.

6. Women who work in high-end clothing boutiques never outgrew playing Barbies. They live to dress and accessorize others.

7. The villainous Jesse James was wrong about me. I am not fat.

8. So there.

The boutique adventure behind us, we head to the mall for the discount version of any one of the great dresses I tried on. I feel remarkably calm and confident, considering where I'm going, and of course, where I have just been. I think I'm ready to buy a dress. A girly, pretty, feminine-but-not-too-obvious dress to wear to Ben's parents' house where I will meet his family. With that thought, things start to change. All my calm and confidence drain away. Chel sees it happening and steers me right to a pretzel counter.

"Here. Fortify." She shoves a hot pretzel into my shaking hand, and I remember again why I love this girl.

"Thanks. It's going to be okay, right?"

She nods. I wonder if she's getting tired of this conversation.

We poke our heads into a few department stores' dress sections and then turn and leave. I can feel my spine going boneless. Where are the magic dresses? How could I have walked out of Fiori Bianchi without buying one of the only dresses that would make me look good enough to accompany Ben to a party? Is it not actually possible to find such fabulous clothing on my stupid budget? Am I going to have to go back to the boutique, concede defeat, and shell out hundreds of dollars? Maybe I can go without groceries. For a few months.

"Aha. There you go," Chel says with the air of a forties film detective solving a particularly lengthy and annoying case. She nods toward a display of dresses under the magic sign: Clearance.

I feel like I ought to at least pretend that this is a risk, but who would I be kidding? There will be something here. There will. I dance over to the rack and grab every single dress in my size, as well as all of them one size up and one size down because I'm such a worldly-wise shopper now.

Behind her straight face, Chel is totally laughing at me. And do I care? No. Well, not right now, anyway.

"On we go. To success, and victory."

# Chapter Eight

All these aunts and uncles! Where did they come from? Does anyone else in the world have so much family? I process exactly three names before I give up, deciding that remembering these people is totally optional. Because what are the odds that I'll ever see any of them again?

Ben's mom is cute. In a completely nonthreatening way, she dishes out smiles and double-handed fist squeezes. She tells me how charming it is to meet me, and then she scoots across the hall to direct the caterers. She could be a character in a romance novel if she was crazy or obsessed or extremely rich, but it looks like she's a totally normal mom.

Here are two more lovely sisters, complete with handsome husbands and gorgeous babies, and probably related to these cute little knee-high people running around sneaking treats. And a brother. Wow. He's as good looking as Ben. He could be Material, too. Not for me, you know. Just in general.

I feel an added level of nervousness now, and I don't think it's about Meeting the Family. My sense of danger is kicking up.

I can feel all kinds of eyes on me. My hair is standing up on the back of my neck. I keep glancing around. My pulse is faster, as if ready to pump up my heart so I can flee whatever horror awaits me. What is the matter with me? Honestly, I don't think Ben's relatives are going to hurt me. What am I all tense about?

Oh, I know.

Ben has a dog.

A big dog.

We've managed to avoid the ridiculous conversation about my dog aversion until now, and I hope we can continue to ignore my condition, but if his dog comes bounding out here and starts leaping up on me and sniffing me and licking my skin, I'm not going to be able to hide the fact that I'm terrified.

I sort of want to ask him where the dog is. I can at least prepare myself for a confrontation if I know from which direction he's likely to come bolting. But if I bring it up, is he going to want to introduce me to the dog, too? I'm pretty sure if I keep my mouth shut and my radar at the ready, I can put Ben between me and the Death Hound if the need should arise.

We stand on his parents' patio, me completely uncomfortable in my knee-length pink (pink!) dress and strappy sandals, him slouching against the railing. Watching the guests wander around the yard, I find the bride. As far as casual elegance goes, Megan is remarkable, even in Ben's beautiful family. Her dress is stunning in its simplicity. Her hair is, I'm thinking, fantastic, when I realize it's in a ponytail. Who else could make a ponytail so fashionable? Understated makeup, three pink rosebuds in her bouquet, gorgeous husband's hand on her back—and she's absolutely the most natural beauty I've ever seen.

What am I doing here?

When she's not making a guest feel lucky to have her

undivided attention, she's glancing up at Will with this obvious adoration that makes me feel like I've stumbled, clumsy and obnoxious, into a private and perfect moment. I almost want to leave, but I'm helpless to tear myself away from all this beauty.

I feel sick to my stomach. Why? Is there something wrong with romantic affection at a wedding reception? Is it that I'm in the middle of a perfect romance novel wedding, complete with flowers and great food, and it's not mine? Well, of course it's not mine. That's crazy. I glance back at Ben and realize that's not it at all. I don't belong here. Not with this elegant group of guests. Not with Ben's oversized family.

Not with Ben.

These past few weeks of studying and playing guitars and hanging out can't last. He's bound to notice sooner or later that this is just the weirdest game. People are going to think there's something between us. Doesn't that mortify him? Maybe he should wear a sign. I could find out when his birthday is and buy him a T-shirt that says, "We're just friends."

I sneak another look back at Ben. There's the strangest look on his face. He's completely intense, with a hint of a smile. He looks like he won some huge prize, but he doesn't want to tell anyone yet. Okay, honestly, it looks like he's checking me out. That is so weird that I feel my neck flush. He smiles and does his "come here" head toss. With absolutely no desire to refuse, I walk over. Taking my hand, he leads me down a flagstone path. My stomach is full of tarantulas. His thumb is tracing a circle on the back of my hand and I'm mentally slapping myself for even fighting it. So what if it's ridiculous? So what if we make no sense together? If something's wrong here, he's the one who's crossing the line. I'm just getting really, really lucky. At that thought, I feel his arm barely grazing my back and we're dancing. He needs to talk now. I have to hear him say something so I know he's still real.

"Mmm. You smell good."

No. Did *I* just say that out loud? No. Oh, please no. Find a hole for me to hide in. Fast.

"Wow, thanks, Sarah. That's sweet. You're not really one to toss around a compliment." He smiles down at me with those eyes—any good romance would call them "come-hither eyes."

I am so hither.

"I wouldn't want it to go to your head," I say, smiling (okay, flirting, I confess).

"I think *you've* gone to my head," he whispers so close to my ear that I feel the words more than hear them.

I sense my mouth hanging slightly open from shock. *Why does he say things like that?* I ask myself.

*Apparently he means it,* I answer.

*He does not mean it. He is just being sweet. It makes no sense.*

*Certainly not, but you should forget that fact and enjoy this— whatever it is—as long as it lasts.*

*But he's Adonis, and I'm . . . Pippi Longstocking.*

*Close your mouth, Pippi. And open your eyes to who is standing here with his arms around you.*

His hand is on my cheek, in my hair, outlining my ear. Is it possible to vomit from pleasure?

*Nice.*

I'm staring at a button on his shirt. I can't hear the music anymore. There's a funny sort of buzzing in my head and then his finger is under my chin, lifting my face. It's suddenly very warm out here. I know etiquette requires me to close my eyes, but I can't stop looking at his face. He brushes my cheek with the side of his face. His nose touches mine. I can feel his breath on my skin as his lips graze across my cheek.

The back of my waist, where his other hand is resting, might burst open to relieve some of this tension in me. I can actually feel my heartbeat in my back. The hand on my face is moving. Gliding. It's gliding under my ear and into the back of my hair. My whole body shivers, even though it's so warm. His fingers run a line from the base of my neck down to my shoulders and I think I might fall over.

"Ben! There you are," a loud voice calls from behind me. The voice is sort of familiar, but wrong, somehow. Too strong. I will myself back to reality. Taking a quick glance at Ben, I shake out of the dream state I've been in and look over my shoulder.

Poof. The dream is over.

It's like a nightmare now.

It's like I've been caught on tape in my ridiculous attempt to fit into my fantasy.

It's worse than I could have imagined.

It's her. Existential Journey Girl. Here, at Ben's parents' house. What is she doing here? How does she know Ben? Why, oh, why is she leaning around me to kiss his cheek? Why is he letting her? Why does he look happy to see her?

"Hi, Kris. This is Sarah. Sarah, this is my cousin, Krissy."

Cousin? She's his *cousin*?

"Hi. We've met. We have a class together," I try to say casually. My mother would be so proud that manners are winning out over the urge to tell Ben the truth. To expose her as the crazy philosophy girl.

She glances at me, and then away, saying nothing.

What a hideous break. Well, at least he didn't choose her. A relative has to be tolerated, I guess. But this doesn't look like tolerance. His face is happy, his shoulders relaxed. He's smiling at her. He's talking to her, but his arm is around me. His fingers rest on my waist and he pulls me tight against his side. There are pieces of this moment I should be enjoying. But *her?* She's a psycho. A poser. A fake.

But she's not acting like a psycho. She's talking in that normal voice. The one she used when she tried to chat me up in class. Her voice is intelligent and confident. She makes eye contact with Ben and she seems to be saying totally normal things. Aside from the fact that she doesn't seem to notice I'm here, she appears completely sane.

They laugh together about some aunt who has a tendency to monitor the food table too closely. She touches his shoulder (the one I'm not standing in front of) as she talks to him. They are totally comfortable. I want to go, but I don't want to draw any attention to myself. She's doing such a good job of ignoring my existence. Besides, if I run away, how do I know I won't accidentally find the hidden dog?

What if she brings up philosophy class? Would she? She's being so . . . normal. She probably wouldn't risk being exposed as one of those fakey girls. What if he figures out that she's the one I've been mocking? Would that hurt his feelings? What about hers? Wait—I don't care about her feelings. But I really don't want to seem like the mean girl. So I'll just stand here and be invisible.

Apparently I'm pretty good at it. She doesn't look at me at all.

# Chapter Nine

**M**orning brings with it all my confused memories of the reception, including the freeze-out by Krissy the Psycho. How am I supposed to feel? How do I know? A part of me is giddy from the almost-kiss with Ben. (We really almost had a kiss, didn't we? I didn't dream that, right?) Then there's the part that's relieved I didn't jump into that particular fire without knowing how to get back out. Because once I go there, into the kissing place, there may be no easy way for me to save myself when things go wrong. Not that there was any real opportunity after Krissy showed up. She didn't leave Ben's side for the rest of the evening. She even rode along when he brought me home. She sat in the backseat. That was weird, like she was a chaperone. Ugh. This is so far from up my alley that I know I need Chel. She agrees to meet me for a smoothie and a muffin.

In a Whirl has all the indispensables: fresh pastries, great smoothies and juice, and a very cute counter boy. Zak is the sixteen-year-old son of John and Bobbie, the owners. He's tall, dark, has nice teeth, and is much too young to be anything but a casual flirt. Chel and I count on finding him Mondays, Tuesdays, and Thursdays when we're in crisis.

"Hi, Sarah. Hi, Chel-bell. What's your pleasure?" Zak smiles.

We order some fabulous concoction that manages to project healthy vibes (even though between us we can, in fact, count calories) and grab a booth near the window. A quiet day like this is rare here, and John and Bobbie both wave from behind the counter.

"So, do tell. Or does this need to wait?" Chel asks.

I give her a pleading, puppy-dog-eye look, and she pats my hand. She understands. Once I start this conversation, I'll need to be able to finish it without interruptions. But I need to start soon. I can feel my foot swinging against the booth's leg, so I tuck my feet under me.

At the risk of implosion, I wait to tell her anything until Zak has delivered our mango smoothies. I don't need to be distracted today. However, distraction is clearly on Zak's mind as he sits in the booth beside Chel.

"What's new, ladies?" He grins.

"Sweetie," Chel responds, giving him her full attention, "you know how we love spending hours of our free time with you. But right now Sarah absolutely must dish. She's having relationship trauma, and I have to tell her how she's supposed to feel. We love your guts. Now get lost. And we need a poppy seed muffin." She plants a kiss in the air near his cheek and elbows him out of the booth.

Not wounded at all, Zak flashes us a charming smile and saunters back to the counter.

Sparing the embarrassing details, I tell her about the reception. I describe me in the dress. She nods, pleased. I tell about the relatives everywhere. As I reach the Near-Kiss, Chel's fingernail thing starts. She has a baffling habit of tapping any solid surface (table, notebook, bus window) with the nail of her left index finger when she's annoyed. Conveniently right-handed, she can nail-tap while taking notes, text messaging, and brushing her teeth.

No sympathy for my embarrassment? No squeal for the almost-kiss? Nope. Just the nail-tap.

"What? What did I do? What's with the finger?" Perplexed, I wait for an explanation.

Chel glances at the offending finger and she stirs her straw in her drink.

Years of friendship have not made me patient enough to outwait a silent moment. "What?" I almost shout.

Glancing around In a Whirl, Chel gives me the look of disapproval I've come to expect. "Do not be surprised, babe, that you have serious relationship issues. This is nothing new for you. I don't know why you even called me. What did you think I would tell you?"

"What are you talking about? What issues?"

"Sarah. Tell me the truth. Would you have let him kiss you? Standing out there in front of a whole wedding reception full of strangers, would you have kissed him?"

Now that is a dumb question. "I—"

"One word. That is all I require. Yes or no. Which is it?"

"You—"

"Yes or no."

"Probably." Then, quietly, honestly, "Not. But it didn't happen. He didn't. We didn't."

"And why not?" Tap, tap, tap.

"I told you, it was the girl—the philosophy nightmare. She

was like a huge leech." As I list all the reasons why there is no actual kiss to report, and why that is all Krissy's fault, I hear the whine rising in my voice. I am actually trying to convince Chel (who knows me better than my mother does and sometimes better than I do) that if there were no Krissy, there would be an official Ben-and-Sarah. Recognizing how ridiculous that is, I do the smart thing and shut up.

"Okay, Chel. Why wouldn't I have kissed him?"

"Do you really want to hear this?"

Honestly? Oh, well . . . "Maybe not. Tell me about your weekend." I need to fortify with cold carbs. Chel silently stares me down as I slurp my smoothie. When I finally put the drink down, she speaks. It's like an interview. If she'd been wearing glasses, she'd be looking at me over the tops of them.

"What's wrong with him, anyway?"

This baffles me. "Nothing. He's perfect."

"That's stupid. Nobody's perfect. He just hasn't uncovered his flaws in front of you yet."

"Says you. He's fantastic."

She shrugs. "We'll see. Anyway, back to the point. You would not have let Ben kiss you in front of a large group of strangers for the following reasons. Number one: You hate people noticing you. That would have been far too conspicuous, especially at a gathering of his entire extended family. And you in that pink dress. Number two: Too many witnesses."

"That's the same thing," I interrupt, waving my hand to erase her comment.

"Not at all. For entirely different reasons, you could not allow these people—even total strangers—to see you with him in case it doesn't work out. You have a deep-seated conviction that you should never be seen in a romantic situation with anyone who will not be your husband."

"That is completely ridiculous."

"You're absolutely right. It *is* ridiculous. You have a ridiculous Prince Charming complex. You won't give any relationship a chance to live because you can't believe it will compare to—"

Is she going to say it out loud? Is someone in this smoothie café going to hear this conversation and know that I read romance novels? That I hope, somewhere in the deep places of my heart, to be able to live that kind of story?

"Chel," I hiss. "Please."

She lowers her voice. "Okay, compared to anything you may have read once. How's that? You won't even give yourself a chance to be a girlfriend because you think you don't fit into your own story."

I'm not sure where this is going, exactly, but I know Chel is wrong. Mostly wrong about the "girlfriend" word. Because I may be a study partner, and I may be a friend, and I may even be a guitar buddy, but I'm not the kind of person who will ever be Ben's girlfriend. I don't mean to suggest that he's doing anything wrong, like leading me on. He has to know that I don't expect any of that . . . that *stuff* he does to mean anything. He's just playing. And I can play along.

A game of Follow the Leader, where he is always the leader.

There's nothing "girlfriend" about me. Ben is a nice guy with a tendency to be affectionate. So he spends a lot of time with me. He has time to spend. So he says nice things. That's because he's a nice guy. So he touches my hair, my face. He's a tactile learner. His family was all touchy, too—big hand shakers, shoulder huggers, and back slappers. They just do that. So what that when he looks right at me, my insides melt. That is totally not his problem. He doesn't mean to do that, and he shouldn't be held responsible for what goes on with me because he happens to be extremely hot.

"Chel, Ben does not want me to be his girlfriend. You are deluded because you love me. And you assume everyone else wants to love me, too. But there is no way Ben wants to be together like that with me. He just likes to hang out."

She looks offended.

"You," she says, pointing her straw at my face, "are an idiot. One of these days, young lady, you are going to have to learn to believe that you're good enough." She looks like my mom when she says that. Like she's humoring me into something. Like she has some stash of Great Wisdom that someday, if I'm extremely lucky, I may get to glimpse. That is so annoying.

I know I'll sound defensive before I even start talking, because my whole head is near exploding with the desire to say "nu-huh, nu-huh" and prove Chel wrong.

"Look, Chel. I know I'm good enough for a lot of things, but there are some lines that girls like me just don't cross. And being the girlfriend to anyone like Ben is an impossibility." I shrug acceptance at the finality of my own logical conclusion.

Her face actually lights up with inspiration. She is having an Aha Moment, right here in the booth. I try to be patient enough to let her share it with me, but no luck. She stares at me with her eyes wide open, and I feel like she's seeing me turned inside out, or without all the proper clothing (and without the benefit of boutique lighting). This does not bring me comfort.

"What? What is it already?" I try not to shout, I really do. But still, my voice is louder than strictly necessary for her to hear me in this booth. I look around, embarrassed to see Zak and both his parents watching us.

"I cannot believe you. This isn't about Ben at all, is it? This is Jesse James holdover," Chel says, in a totally appropriate tone of voice. "You're keeping some preset distance from Ben because of that loser, aren't you?"

I almost try to deny this, but what would be the point? She knows. So I shrug.

"Just because Jesse was a jerk, and he made you feel like an idiot, you're going to pass this up?"

"What is there to pass up? Ben doesn't feel that way about me."

She stares at my face for a minute, maybe waiting for me to change my mind. But there's no changing the facts.

"The events of last night might suggest otherwise," she says.

Shaking my head, I brace myself to reopen a heavily padlocked door. "Apparently we could be mistaken about a guy's intentions. Again."

I actually feel myself growing shorter as memories of the nefarious Jesse crowd heavily on my shoulders. He acted interested. He followed my lead. He let me believe—*made* me believe—that he was interested, even attached. Then he dropped me on my face, right in front of the whole watching world.

Chel takes my hand from across the booth. "He's the one who was wrong. Not us. We read him perfectly. He liked you. He acted like a boyfriend because he *was* the boyfriend. Then he got stupid and changed his mind. Then he said really mean and hurtful things to try and make himself look better when he decided he wasn't interested."

Then she says this: "But Ben *is* interested, and that's going to rock your world."

I pretend not to hear her.

# Chapter Ten

C an I come home with you after study group?" Ben asks during Novetsky's Friday lecture. He slouches down in his chair, and since I'm sitting on my feet, he is looking up at me. That feels weird, since he's so much taller than I am.

"Sure. Can I make you dinner? Or is that too late to eat?"

He sits up, leans close and whispers, "Early or late, eating is always a good idea." His breath in my ear turns my stomach to jelly.

I'm sure he's just being nice. And who doesn't like food? But when he starts tracing my fingers, I forget about food. Why is he always touching me? Maybe he's just a guy who's comfortable touching. But I am not used to that, and I can't hear a word of the lecture over the rushing of blood in my ears.

I glance down to see the TA sprawled out in his seat by the screen. There is no doubt that he is still among the hottest guys at this university, but I haven't noticed so much lately. I'm being distracted all over the place, here.

Study group is going to be a joke if I don't take some notes pretty soon. Keeping my right hand on the armrest between us, I peck out some names and dates with my left index finger. I feel like Chel—tap, tap, tap. Except I'm not annoyed. Just overwhelmed.

"Do you need this?" Ben whispers, picking up my hand.

"I'm taking pretty lame notes without it," I admit.

"How about this—I will remember every word for study group tonight if you let me keep this." He laces my fingers through his.

I can't help smiling as I look down at the screen and tap out another date. Date. I like that word. As in I have a date for dinner tonight.

Walking back to my apartment, Ben takes my hand again. I shiver, and I think it's from the chilly air. I've decided to keep living in the moment and just go with it. That way, if he ever decides to do the math and realize that he could do better, at least I won't have been the one making the moves.

"You were awesome at study group," I tell him. He led the discussion, with no notes—straight out of his memory—as though he had heard every word of today's lecture and not been distracted in the least. I choose to see that as a good thing.

"Well, thanks. I figure it's time to prove that I'm not as dumb as I look." He glances over at me, waiting. He expects me to say something.

"You don't look dumb." I wish I could say the rest. The parts that go, *You look witty and surprising and gorgeous and strong and handsome and sensitive and gentle and remarkable and carefree and just thoroughly hot.* But I can't say those words. I will never be able to say those words. So I leave it at the half-compliment and wish I could do better.

He gives a little head-shake. "So," he asks, changing the subject, "what are we eating tonight?"

"Do you like Indian food?" I ask. He looks slightly alarmed. "You know, curry?" Now he looks like he's trying not to look alarmed.

"Hey, sure. I'm up for anything," he says. But his tone implies otherwise. I'd love to keep teasing, really make him sweat, but I can't.

"Okay. Someday I'll make you an awesome curry. But tonight, how about chicken parmesan?"

Such a look of relief crosses his face that I have to laugh.

"I guess Italian is a little more my style," he confesses.

When we reach my apartment, I peek through the slats on the window blinds and then turn my back to the door. He deserves a warning; I know I would have liked one. "Okay. Here's the thing. I have this roommate who has a boyfriend. He spends a lot of time over here, specifically on the couch. I haven't ever actually seen his face because he's generally very busy with all the making out. They are in there right now, and so here's the plan. We walk through, go straight to the kitchen, and forget what's happening in the living room. Are you okay with that?"

Why is he laughing? This is no joke.

"I'm totally okay with that."

When we open the door, I say hi, and Mandy extracts one arm to wave hello. Ben and I head through to the kitchen. "So that's Mandy," I say. "She's a pretty nice girl if you can get her alone. Not that that's likely to happen."

I preheat the oven. If Ben knew anything about cooking, he'd know I spent most of this afternoon preparing this meal.

I'm glad he doesn't know. It would probably seem kind of forward of me. I am so determined not to be forward with him, ever, in our nice little game of Follow the Leader, where I am never It. But I will impress him with dinner, tonight and as often as possible.

While the chicken is cooking and the sauce is heating, I ask Ben to help me make the salad. He gives me a blank look. I toss him a head of Romaine, and he stares, first at it, then at me. Handing him a colander, I reach up for a bowl. He stands there, holding the lettuce and looking lost.

"Um, Sarah? Maybe I don't know how to make salad. Unless it comes in a bag. Help."

"Stay close. The mysteries of the universe are about to unfold."

He follows me to the sink, where I break off a few leaves of lettuce and toss them into the strainer. He watches me rinse off the leaves and shake the water into the sink.

"Okay. Small pieces. Bite-sized. Into the bowl." Baby steps. He reaches for a knife, but I stop him. "Tear it with your hands. The knife will make it rusty."

When I see that he's handling the lettuce part, I start rummaging through the fridge. "Do you like tomatoes? Cucumbers? Carrots? Red onions? Yellow peppers? Peas? Hard-boiled egg? How about cheese?"

"All of the above. Except maybe no peas. And we need croutons. That's my favorite part."

While I slice carrots and peppers, Ben talks about study group. I'm determined to hear every word this time. No more getting distracted by the fact that Ben exists. Here. In my kitchen. Mutilating an onion.

"Will you check the sauce for me?"

He looks panicked.

"It's in the saucepan on the stove. Just take off the lid and give it a stir."

He's very obedient, even though I can tell he's nervous that he's going to mess it up somehow. "Mmm. That smells great," he says. *His first yummy-sounds,* I notice. "This one's breathing steam." He points to the pot.

"It's boiling. Want to put the pasta in? Just like making mac and cheese," I tease.

I show him how much to put in, and he handles it just fine. He offers to set the table. I grab plates and glasses and show him where the utensils live. He starts folding napkins into fancy shapes.

"We go out to a lot of restaurants. I may not know how to boil water, but I can make an awesome napkin swan," he says.

I set the food out and carry the plates over to the table. I'm pleased. It looks beautiful.

"Great job on the salad. I can't wait to eat it." I smile at him.

"Wow. This looks great. You should charge for this. You'd make a fortune."

"Maybe you ought to taste it before you have any more big ideas," I say.

He picks up his napkin, making a production out of unfolding it onto his lap. I wait for him to start eating. He cuts a little bite of chicken, wraps up a strand of pasta, scoops it through the sauce, and puts it in his mouth. His eyes widen, then close. He chews slowly. For a long time. Is the chicken tough? I scramble to cut a bite. No. It's perfect.

"Wow. That is nice," he says, opening his eyes.

I smile and feel my shoulders relax. I realize that I really want him to be impressed. I want him to think I do good things. I want him to think about me when he eats good food.

"Mmm. Sarah, that is awesome."

I haven't eaten another bite. It's too fun to sit here and watch him eat, listen to his yummy-sounds. Hear him say my name.

"How did we do on the salad?" he asks.

I take a bite. Pretend to weigh my decision. I mean, it's salad.

"It's very good. You're a pro." I'm flattering him. I'm flirting. I'm okay with that.

He finishes his chicken and looks over at the stove.

"Sorry," I say. "There are two of us. I made two servings. That's all there is."

"But it was so good," he sort of moans.

"Here, you can have some of mine," I offer, stabbing a bite on my fork. I hold it across to him. He looks conflicted. Maybe it's gross that I put it on my fork. Maybe he has a germ thing. Then he seems to get over it, whatever it was. He takes my hand and pulls the fork up to his mouth. His lips close over the bite of chicken, and he slides the fork out of his mouth. My fingers start to sweat. I'm about to put that fork back into my mouth. The thought gives me tiny shivers on my neck. I cut myself another bite. He's picking at his salad. The chicken really is very good, and I'm so glad. I want him to dream about this tonight.

"You need another bite. Here, slide your plate over." I cut what remains of my chicken in half and slip it onto his plate. He tries (not very hard) to say no. "I can always make more," I remind him.

"Really? Right now?" he says. His face lights up like Christmas.

I fake a stern, mother-ish voice. "No, because then you won't want any dessert. And it's chocolate."

He puts his hands on his heart. "You made me dessert?"

"Finish your chicken. And then we have to do the dishes. And *then* you can have dessert," I tell him. He laughs and shovels his remaining chicken into his mouth in one bite.

"That was so good, Sarah. You are a woman of many talents."

I roll my eyes. He's right, of course, but he's also kind. "Do you want to sit right there and tell me a story while I do the dishes? It'll only take me a minute."

"How about I tell you a story while I help you do the dishes? Then we can be done in half a minute."

"That's very charming. Do you know any half-minute stories?"

"I'm full of them. I'll rinse; you stack." He stands beside me at the sink. It's a pretty small kitchen. Our elbows knock into each other. I don't mind.

Ben starts his story. "Once, when I was a kid we went to visit Uncle Steve. He lives on a farm in Iowa. He had baby lambs. He let me climb through the fence and pick one up. I was scared to death. I thought it would bite me. Or maybe its mom would charge, and it'd be in the newspaper—Maniac Sheep Attack. But when I finally got my courage up to hold it, I loved it. I sat in the dirt with that lamb on my lap for hours, just stroking its curly hair and feeling it breathe. I wanted to bring it home with me. My mom thought that was a really bad idea. She said that if I wanted to, I could sleep in the barn, though. That turned out to be way too scary because there were spiders in the barn. So my mom took a picture of me holding the little lamb, and I put it in a frame in my room. It's still there."

"Did I meet Uncle Steve at the reception?"

"No, he didn't come. Actually, he's not really my uncle. He's one of a whole bunch of people who aren't actually related to us. My parents' old friends from college, sometimes people they used to work with, people like that. I guess it's lame, but I like having all these fake relatives. It gets us out on trips around the country, because we have people to stay with just about everywhere."

"Where's the best place you've visited a fake relative?"

"Charleston, South Carolina. Have you ever been there?"

I've never been anywhere. I shake my head. "What was great about it?"

"Well, the ocean. And the hairy trees." He sees my questioning look and clarifies. "The trees have this spooky, hairy moss dangling off them. It's like in a ghost story. And it's scary to drive through these forests in a rainstorm. The city is really cool. It has stone streets and all this great food, and musicians and vendors all over the place. And Aunt Jo and Uncle Joe."

"I know you're making that up."

He laughs a little and shakes his head. "Honest. He's Joseph and she's Joleen. They're hilarious. We went the summer after Megan graduated, so it was just me and my parents and the Joes. I loved hanging out at their house with their daughter. She is—I was going to say cute, but that's not really good enough. She's kind of miraculous. She has the prettiest eyes I've ever seen, and this soft, beautiful hair that's almost white because she's out in the sun all the time."

I'm starting to feel squirmy, and I'd like to change the subject, but he presses on.

"She was so excellent about having us come and stay. It seemed like we didn't get in her way at all. She made me feel at home, introduced me around the neighborhood and all that, and we were like best friends right away. We were totally comfortable together. By the second day, she was climbing into my lap and kissing my face."

Wow. What a tramp. What in the world am I supposed to say to that? I try to hide my face, because there's no way he won't be able to tell exactly how uncomfortable this little stroll down memory lane has made me feel.

"Did I mention that she was four?"

I level a serious glance at him and say, "You're not that funny, you know." But he is, and I can't help laughing with him as he scrubs out the saucepan. Dishes finished, we sit back at the table.

"Did you always want to come to school here?" My turn to play the part of the interviewer.

"It's not such a big deal to me, but it is to my family. My dad started working for the university when I was really little. My brother and sisters all got their degrees here, so it's sort of a family tradition. Everyone was relieved when I was accepted." He's looking at the table, nervous.

"What do you mean?" Am I being nosy?

"I'm"—he hedges around for a second—"not that good at school stuff."

"Sure you are. You were awesome at study group," I remind him.

"Memorizing is okay. I can do that." He looks up and smiles like he's changing the channel on this discussion. Hooking his feet around the legs of the chair I'm sitting on, he pulls it closer to him.

"Dinner was completely fantastic. But it's been more than ten minutes, and I'm hungry again. How about this dessert I keep hearing about?"

"Are you actually hungry?" I ask, surprised.

He shrugs. "Not really, but I want to know what you made. You said the word *chocolate*. And who says you have to be hungry to want to eat dessert?"

He really has the greatest smile. I need to remember my rules, or I might act like that South Carolina girl and climb into his lap and kiss his face.

I give myself a little distance and head to the fridge for dessert. I set a dish of chocolate mousse in front of Ben and hand him a spoon.

He dips in and takes a bite. With a very serious look on his face, he says, "Sarah, please. Please tell me you made more."

I laugh at him. The front door opens and closes, but I don't hear anyone talking or coming in. I wait a minute and peek around the corner. Mandy and the Faceless One have left.

"That was quick. And quiet. How do you know if they're here or gone?" Ben says as he finishes his mousse.

"Oh, yeah," I say sarcastically, "they're totally subtle."

"Ninjas," he suggests, and I laugh again as I picture Mandy and her boyfriend dressed head to toe in black, concealing all kinds of deadly weapons in their pant legs and under their shoes. Weapons they'll never use, because they're way too busy kissing.

We head into the now-vacant living room. I make sure to sit on the couch that Mandy and her boyfriend were not using, because it would feel too weird to sit on the one they'd warmed up so energetically. Ben sits right beside me.

"What's your favorite holiday?" And he's back to the interview. This could go on forever.

"The Fourth of July. Want to know a secret?" I whisper, but not like *that*, not like I need him to lean into me.

He nods and scoots a little closer to me on the couch.

"I love to set things on fire. I love the smell of matches and fireworks. I used to make little bonfires in my backyard out of twigs and leaves. My mom would get so mad—she was sure I was going to burn the house down. But I never did. Not even close. I was always totally careful. I'd plan for where the wind was blowing."

"I definitely believe that part. You are the most careful person I know. I bet you plan everything. You probably know what you're going to wear tomorrow, don't you?"

I shrug. (Yes. My favorite jeans and a brown short-sleeved sweater. None of your business.)

"So do things usually go according to your plans?" he wants to know.

"That depends. And I don't plan everything. If I did, it would be hard to live with roommates. I can't plan for what anyone else is going to do. Especially the crazy people."

"But do you plan how you'll react to certain situations? Like tonight? Did you know what you'd do if your roommate was making out in the living room?"

"Well, yeah, but that's almost a given around here. I'm actually amazed that you've never been in the same room with her before. I'm not sure either one of them is actually enrolled in classes. That couch is theirs most nights, and some afternoons, Saturdays, and holidays. It's part of life to work around Mandy. But I didn't really have to plan anything, because I knew that if they were in the apartment, they would be on the couch. We could walk through and pretend not to notice them. It's not like I would have to figure out what to do about dinner if they were in the kitchen. They don't eat. They don't drink. I'm not even sure they speak to each other. It's not a very complex relationship."

"So basically what you're saying is that yes, you do have a plan for everything."

"You say that as if it's a bad thing." I'm laughing with him.

"So what are you planning to do if I reach over there and hold your hand?"

"Why?" I ask. "Do you think I'm going to pull it away? Are you worried?"

Ben shakes his head. "Not about holding your hand. What are you planning to do if I touch your hair?"

I duck my head a little. "Probably squirm. My hair is so out of control."

He takes a breakaway curl and spins it around his finger. I hold as still as a statue.

"What about if I touch your face?" he asks.

"I have to be honest with you, that isn't one I've planned for." My words come out a little broken, because I'm suddenly having trouble breathing correctly.

He reaches over and strokes the side of my face with his fingers. A shiver runs from the top of my hair all the way down my arms. I turn my face into his touch. Well, I didn't plan that. His face is very close to mine. I'm having flashbacks to the wedding reception.

"What are you planning to do when I kiss you?" he whispers into my neck.

Does he expect me to answer that? Wait, did he say *when* I kiss you, or *if* I kiss you? Oh, when. And when is right now. His mouth meets mine for a very short second, and he pulls back, just as I lean in closer. I lose any remaining sense of balance and almost fall into him.

He catches my face in both his hands. He smiles at me and holds my face, and I feel dizzy, but in a good way. I put my hand on the couch behind his shoulder to steady myself. He slides an arm around my back; the other hand is in my hair, right at the base of my neck. My spine dissolves and I'm not at all sure how I manage to stay upright.

He pulls me closer and kisses me again. My hand moves from the couch to his shoulder, and then into his hair. I'm melting, and I need to hold onto something so I don't end up on the floor at his feet. I wrap my fingers around his hair and clutch.

This is a totally new experience for me, kissing Ben. So why does it seem so familiar? Maybe because he tastes like chocolate mousse. Maybe because I'm getting used to the smell of him. No. It's the sounds. The noise I'm hearing—the noise I'm making. *Yummy-sounds.* I've given myself up to the thrill of the moment, just like during a perfect meal. The realization makes me want to laugh. That certainly isn't planned. What would he say if I laughed?

If I laugh, though, he will stop kissing me. I absolutely must not laugh. Because no matter the point of this game we're playing, I am winning.

## Chapter Eleven

I drag myself out of bed after nine. I should really go for a walk, or do something useful, but I think I'd rather sit around and relive the events of last night.

Ben's hands on my hair. Ben, kissing me. Me, kissing him back.

That really happened, didn't it?

Wow.

I stretch my arms and scratch my crazy hair as I slouch into the kitchen. Lauren is there.

"Morning," I chirp. Wow. If I weren't me, I'd hate me for that unnecessary burst of cheeriness.

She points to the table. There's a box wrapped in brown paper. "Package for you," she says.

This is a momentous occasion. Both my first package delivered at school, and the first words Lauren has ever aimed toward me.

"Cool. Who's it from?" She obviously knows that this is a rhetorical question, because she doesn't bother to answer. I call out "See ya," to her retreating back. She pauses and waves without turning around.

I'm feeling pretty great about our little communication breakthrough.

The box is from my mom. I'd know it even if I hadn't seen her postmark or her handwriting, because she's the only person I know under the age of eighty who uses that sticky brown tape with the string in it. Does she think someone's going to try to secretly open this package and then reseal it without leaving a trace? Fat chance.

I rummage around in the drawer for a steak knife that can defeat the tape. Inside the box are a bag of oatmeal-butterscotch cookies and a book. No note. Well, she made cookies, so I know she put some time and effort into this, even if she couldn't be bothered to write a letter to go along with it. I pull out three cookies for breakfast. Hey, there's oatmeal in there. That's totally a breakfast food.

And the book—this is an unusually thoughtful thing for my mom to do. It's my well-worn, warped-spine copy of Shel Silverstein's *Where the Sidewalk Ends.* Fanning through the poems, I can identify spots of raspberry sherbet and grass stains, and the seventeen wavy pages from the time I let part of the book fall into the bathtub. Technically it's my mom's book. She got it long before I was born, but I loved it and sort of adopted it.

I sit at the table, munching cookies and laughing at poems and drawings. I don't even know how long I've been sitting when there's a knock at the door.

"It's open," I sing out, and the unaccustomed cheer sounds good on me.

Then I realize that it could be anyone at the door.

Or worse, it could be Ben.

Bingo.

It's ten o'clock in the morning, and I'm sitting at the kitchen table in my pajamas, reading kids' poetry, and eating cookies. Well, not eating cookies anymore. I seem to have devoured the entire bag.

He walks through to the kitchen and sits backward on the chair beside me.

"Hey. What are you doing?"

Glancing around, I check if there's any way to pretend I'm actually doing anything at all. Nope. Busted.

"My mom sent a package. Cookies and a book. Favorite book"—I hold it up—"and favorite cookies." I motion lamely to the bag, which doesn't seem to have even crumbs in it anymore. "I'm going to run and clean up. I'll be fast. Here," I shove the book at him, "you can experience my childhood for a few minutes."

He smiles at me, but in that cute, confused way. Does he think I'd stay in this room with him now? I haven't even brushed my teeth yet.

I run to the shower and speed-wash everything. When I get dressed, I actually take a second to consider the clothes I put on. As I shake out my hair, I think for the first time in a long time that I like this mop. At least I don't have to do anything to it to make it look like it looks every other day.

Back in the kitchen, Ben has his feet up on a chair and my book in his hands. He hasn't heard me, so I stand at the doorway and watch him. He's so intense, eyebrows pushed together, absorbing the wonder of the poems, I guess. Then a grin crosses his face and he looks up.

"This is funny." He smiles at me.

"Which one are you on?"

He shows me the page, and I recite the poem to him. He looks impressed. Right on. If he's going to be impressed by children's poems, I'll bring them on.

"You know all these by heart?"

"Not all of them, anymore. But I used to. I read this book about a million times when I was little." I slide into the empty chair and put up my feet next to Ben's. "Read me one."

He shakes his head.

"Come on, please?" I think about fluttering my eyelashes, but I'm not sure that would work.

"No. You read to me." He smiles, but it doesn't look like he means it.

"Come on, just one."

"I'm not reading to you." His tone is different now. Defiant, and a little defensive. And sort of scary. "I don't read out loud." He slides the book across the table to me, a little harder than necessary.

I shrug my shoulders. "Okay, forget it." But I'm not going to forget that. I flip through the book for a second, a little too creeped out to say anything to Ben. Or even to look at him. I've never seen him like this. It's like he's mad, but what would he be mad about?

A long minute goes by.

"Let me see it again," he says in a very quiet voice. He stands up and taps my feet off the chair, scoots it closer to me, and sits down. He has this look of intense determination on his face as he slides his arm around my chair and tilts the book toward him a little.

He takes a slow breath and holds his finger to the page.

"If." Pause. Then, "You." Another pause. "Are a"—long, excruciating pause—"dream . . . dreamer."

I have never regretted anything in my life, every Jesse James moment included, as much as I regret asking Ben to read to me. My scalp is steaming under my wet hair. Humiliation settles around us like a dark fog.

I don't know what to say. That was painful. I keep my eyes on the page.

"I'm not stupid."

I stare at him, and I think my mouth is open.

"I'm not stupid," he repeats.

I shake my head until I can speak. "I know you're not." I do know that. He's got a great memory, and his answers are smart. He does well in classes. But what's with the reading? I have never heard anything so painful. I'd love to find out without actually asking, but how?

Standing up, he holds out his hand. "Want to take a walk?"

"Sure. Let me grab a jacket." My hair is still wet. It's starting to feel chilly outside these days. I'm going to get such a cold for this. But I'm a little scared of Ben right now, and I don't want to tick him off. What did I start here?

He holds the door open for me. When I get to the bottom of the stairs, I wait for him to catch up. Is he going to explain all this to me? He has his hands shoved into his jacket pockets. We walk in quiet, except I keep sniffing from the cool air. Several blocks later, neither of us has said anything. I scour my brain, trying to think of something safe to say, something that won't bring up any uncomfortable subjects. I've got nothing.

"It's just a reading thing," he says out of nowhere, startling me a little. "And a spelling thing. That's why I'm not so great at school stuff, you know. Like I told you."

I'm not at all sure what I'm supposed to say, so I keep my

hands shoved into my pockets too. Watching the sidewalk, I nod.

We walk a few more blocks before he speaks again. "Sorry if that freaked you out. It's not something I was planning to discuss."

"No, I'm not freaked out." Total lie. "No big deal."

"Really?" He sounds so hopeful. He stops me and turns me toward him. Leaving his hands on my shoulders, he sort of half-holds me and looks right at my face. I work hard to look casual. "You're okay about this?"

Okay about what? I don't even know what this is. "Sure." It's so obvious that this is what he wants to hear.

He wraps his arms around my back and squeezes. In relief he leans down and kisses me, fast and happy. Taking my hand now, he moves us down the street again. And apparently that's it. His little bout of moodiness is over, and he's back to telling his stories.

I mostly listen while he tells me about being way behind as a kid in elementary school. "Letters just wouldn't line up for me." The other kids would tease him, call him stupid, give him a bad time. I sort of tune out as he describes his mom's concern and all the visits to doctors. Mainly I hear his voice, his relief that he can talk about this, now, to me. It's weird; it's like he's the girl, wanting to be all emotionally open. I hear the word "dyslexia," and the way it rolls out of his mouth like a polished stone, practiced and comfortable.

*Isn't he embarrassed?*

*Maybe he's used to it. He's had years to adjust, right?*

*Yeah, but it's a learning disability. With a name, a title. I'd die of shame.*

*That's because all you have is your brain.*

*Yeah, no kidding.*

*And he's got everything—looks, talent, athletic ability.*

*What, that's all?*

*Ha, ha.*

He keeps talking. Words crash against my ears, uncomfortable words like "therapy" and "resource aide" and "tutor" and "specialists." My brain connects study-group Caleb with the tutoring part, and I finally realize how Ben and Caleb knew each other. Caleb is Ben's tutor. He is paid (or maybe he volunteers out of the goodness of his depressed heart) to help Ben with his classes. That sounds so humiliating. But Ben seems okay with it all.

We end up at a park where the leaves are bright red and yellow and orange. "I'll push you, if you want," he says as he holds a cracked rubber swing for me.

I sit down on it, and he stands behind me. He gives me a shove, and I stretch my feet out in front of me. When was the last time I did this? I float back to him, but instead of pushing again, Ben stops the swing in front of himself. He holds me against his chest; my head is right in front of his. I think I might fall out on my face. He nuzzles the back of my neck, under my hair, and I know I'm going to fall out now. Chills shoot down my back, but not from the air. He pushes the swing away again, higher this time, and I feel my stomach swoop out from under me. Was that swing-induced, or Ben-induced? Either way, it makes me dizzy.

I'm glad I'm in the swing, because I need a few more minutes to settle my brain. The fact is that Ben is not what I thought he was. I mean perfect. He's not perfect. I know this should make me feel better, so why doesn't it? Why do I have that little creepy feeling? I feel guilty. What is that all about? Is it because I don't have a reading problem and he does? Is it guilt that I know more about him than he knows about me? Or am I just learning not to trust my impressions, again?

Chel walks into my apartment. Ben and I are sitting on the floor, knees touching, playing our guitars. He's teaching me a new song, and I must look pretty intense, because Chel doesn't say anything. She flops onto the couch and puts her feet up. She listens for a while with her eyes closed, enjoying us. I am enjoying us too. Feet bouncing to the rhythm, she stays quiet for a few songs before she spills her great idea.

"I have this great idea. You guys should play at my party on Thanksgiving weekend. Just for an hour or two. Wouldn't that be fun?"

I sit up straighter and rub the tension out of my neck, making way for all-new tension. "You mean like, be the entertainment?" The thought sort of flips my stomach. No way.

"You know," Ben tells her, "we don't really do party kind of stuff. Just this." He strums his guitar in that spine-melting, casual acoustic-hotness way of his.

"*This* is what I want. More like background music. And its not just you. I have another band or two playing. You could take a turn."

Ben looks excited. Is he considering doing this? And what's all this about another band? Who is the first band? Us? Is she kidding?

"What do you think, Sarah? Want to do it?" His face is lit up, eyes shining.

How do I say that I absolutely do not want to have anything

to do with this ridiculous scheme? No, no, no. What words can I use that will convince him that this is not only a bad idea, but a really, really good way to look like an idiot in front of dozens—possibly hundreds—of strangers? No. No. NO.

He looks at me with the most adorable puppy-dog face.

No. No.

He takes my hand and wiggles his eyebrows at me.

No.

He leans over and whispers in my ear, "Hey, I know what. Let's play music together for Chel's party, Sarah. It will be so great. You will be so fantastic. We'll be the greatest guitar duo ever. Come on, let's be the band."

It feels like there's a live snake in my stomach, and I honestly can't tell if it's from his breathing in my ear or from the terrifying suggestion that we play Chel's party.

"Please?" he whispers again and kisses me under the ear.

No. I don't want to. No.

"Okay, I'm in." Who said that? Was that me? Aw, man. That *was* me.

"Great. You guys will be awesome." Chel grins. "I'm leaving now so you can practice." Pause. "I mean practice playing music on your guitars." Can she see my face flaming from there? I think so, because her smile says she can see right into my shallow soul. "Thanks," Chel tosses over her shoulder as she heads out the door.

## Chapter Twelve

The Boss pokes her head into the proofreading cube.

"Who is planning to stay in town for Thanksgiving?" she asks.

"I am," a bunch of us say together. I'm glad I'm not the only one who has no real reason to go home. Mom and Dad have booked a trip to a Native American sweat lodge for the weekend. Mom said something about wanting to celebrate the true roots of the holiday. Whatever.

The Boss thins her lips into a line and shakes her head. "Hands, please."

Maura, Tandy, Dean, and I raise our hands, looking at each other with concealed laughter.

"Very good. Who wants extra shifts during that time?"

Maura, Tandy, and Dean raise their hands again. I look over at Shari. She blushes. I nudge her chair with my foot and whisper, "Are you going home for Thanksgiving?"

She nods. I realize that I don't know where her home is.

"Driving or flying?"

"Driving. With Logan." A smile that must have been buried deep in there starts to escape her face. Shari is absolutely glowing. Her guy is coming home with her for a long weekend—home to meet her family—and she looks startled by her own good fortune. A sudden realization hits my two brains.

*Shari is living her romance.*

*As she should be.*

*Yeah, but she's a . . .*

*What? What are you going to accuse sweet little Shari of?*

*Nothing, except being sweet and little—and maybe the office nerd.*

*So?*

*So she's her own leading lady anyway.*

*Is there any reason she shouldn't be?*

*Well, no. But she's kind of . . . not quite . . . you know. And if she can be her own leading lady, then why not . . . ?*

*Just do it. Finish that thought.*

*Nope.*

*But you're thinking it, aren't you? You're thinking that there's no reason you can't be the heroine in your own story. If Ben's choosing you, you can be chosen.*

*Not listening.*

*Well, you should be. You should be listening, and you should be the leading lady in your own life, and you should be chosen. You should definitely be chosen.*

*Wow. Thanks.*

"Break time," the Boss calls over her shoulder as she marches out of the cubicle.

"And she's off," mutters Maura. "No doubt to practice her routine for 'Stand Up, Sit Down,' the great television comedy sensation that's sweeping the nation."

105

Dean actually laughs at that one. And then he looks repentant.

We move toward the vending machine like robots, giving no thought to what we're doing. But I start talking before we get there.

"So Shari's going home, but you guys are staying here, right?" Nods from Dean, Tandy, and Maura. "Okay, so who wants to come to a party that Friday night?"

Maura looks interested. "What kind of party are we talking about?"

"Totally legal, with no substances more addictive than caramel brownies." I want to make it clear that Chel isn't throwing any party that's going to land anyone in trouble—or in jail.

Maura rolls her black-painted eyes. "I mean, will there be lots of people? Lots of food? Live music?"

I try to look confident and cheerful. "Yes, yes, and yes. And it's funny you should mention the music," I say as I feel the smile leaking off my face. My shoulders suddenly slump and my stomach hurts. "She has a few locals playing an hour at a time. And one of them is me." I must look absolutely dejected now.

I force myself to stand up straight to see if any of them are laughing at me. All three girls are staring at me, openmouthed. Dean is nodding, like maybe he expected as much. Liar.

Tandy is the first to recover from her shock. "You're in a band?" She stresses each word equally, so I can't tell which surprises her more, the "me" part or the "band" part.

I shrug. "It's not really a band, it's just me and my . . . friend. Ben."

Shari puts out her hand to stop me. "Wait. Wait a minute. Ben? Ben the Greek god from your study group?"

I feel my skin heating up. I nod.

"How could you not mention that you're playing music with him, you know, professionally?" She looks like a reporter. She ought to have a microphone in my face, or at least a pencil behind her ear.

"Okay, first of all, no one's getting paid so it's not professional. Second of all, we just hang out and play music together, and third, my friend heard us, and she wants us to play her party. No big deal."

Tandy is shaking her head with a pitying look on her face. "I could never do that. There is no way. You are so brave."

"Or stupid," I concede. I decide to tell them the truth. "I didn't want to do it. I'm terrified. But Ben was so excited, and he sort of used unnecessary force to push me into it."

Shari can't let that one go by. "What did he do?"

I glance at Dean to see if he's going to laugh at me. The poor guy must be way out of his comfort zone here. "He asked really nicely, and then he looked at me with those melty eyes, and then he kissed me. I was helpless. I have no spine. I couldn't say no. He wanted to play the party more than I wanted to not to."

"Did you just say 'to not to'?" Maura laughed. "He's got your head all turned around."

Shari nods as if she's got the measure of it all, now. "You can't go splashing through puddles of happy without getting some of it on you." Tandy and Maura and I stare at her, startled by her poetic gem of wisdom.

"So what you're saying is that you're playing music with your boyfriend at a Thanksgiving weekend party and you want us to come support you," Dean sums up with all the male detachment in the world.

"Pretty much, except not the boyfriend part," I say.

They snort. All of them. And all of them shake their heads.

"What?"

"Are you kidding? He hangs out at your house playing songs on his guitar and kissing you, and you won't call him your boyfriend? That's dumb." Dean's male perspective is quickly losing its detachment.

I look to Shari. She's wide-eyed now. "Get a little confident. Call it what it is. Ben is your dream guy—and now he's your boyfriend. Do you have any idea how rare that is?"

I shake my head. It's not rare. It's impossible. At least for me. "He's just being nice."

Dean steps closer and looks right at me. "No. I'm being nice. I'm not calling you an idiot or accusing you of leading this guy on. I'm nice. He's the boyfriend."

Tandy nods. "Boyfriend."

"Yup," agrees Maura.

Standing there, sinking under the intensity of their collective judgment, I remember the last group of people I had this sort of conversation with. And about whom: The infamous, nefarious, evil Jesse James. Except I was the one using the word "boyfriend" then. And the other people were doing the denying part.

I remember specifically saying the words, "I'm busy tonight. I have plans with my boyfriend." To which McCall Houston, she of the insincere smile and the pretend concern, responded, "You have a boyfriend? How cute. Who is he? Do we know him?" The locker room felt warm, bright and cheery for the first time ever that day.

"Yeah. Jesse. We're dating." I even remember the confidence that accompanied the blush to my face. I was sure it gave me one of those healthy glows that vigorous romance-novel ladies get when they do some unusually robust exercise, like wading across the stream with their skirts pulled over their knees, or returning the runaway horse to its owner and refusing a reward.

McCall Houston managed to evaporate the blush, the confidence, and all the good feelings with her next comment. "You must mean a Jesse from a different school, because I know you aren't dating Jesse Chandler." And then came that famous smile—the one every girl on the outside of McCall's group knew and feared. The "Don't Trust This Smile" smile.

Somehow I managed to keep putting on my shoes, but my brain would not process her comment instantly. "No, yeah. It's Jesse Chandler. We've been going out for a few weeks."

And then she laughed. McCall Houston looked right at me and laughed. Not even pretending to be sincere anymore, right in front of a locker room full of her friends and clinger-on-ers, she said, "Jesse isn't dating you. He is not your boyfriend. He calls you because he wants you to help him with his homework. And don't even ask how I know. He told me. He tells everyone. He wouldn't be dating you, anyway, because he's already dating Brianne Somersby."

There was a lot of unkind laughter then, the kind that hides behind painted nails. I wanted to deny it. I wanted to stand up to her. But I knew I didn't need to. Jesse would stand beside me. Because, come on, Brianne? McCall couldn't have picked a more obvious lie. Jesse would never go out with a girl like Brianne. She was such a poser. She was a completely different person around boys than she was with girls. With girls, she laughed out loud. Near guys, it was all lowered lashes and soft giggles. With girls, she was funny and crazy. With guys, she'd barely speak, just toss her hair and wait for someone to say something that would put the attention back on her. And when she did speak, she said everything in a breathy whisper. That whisper that made guys lean closer to hear her.

I hurried into my school clothes, slowing only to make sure everything that needed to be fastened was fastened. A quick glance in the mirror showed me that nothing strange was hanging out for the whole school to see. For a girl who hated to run, I made a fast trip to Señora Montague's Spanish classroom. I knew Jesse had Spanish next, and I needed to see him, to talk to him. To have him put his arms around me.

But when I got to the classroom door, I noticed that his arms were busy.

And so were his lips. They seemed very occupied. Without even bothering to duck around a corner, he stood outside the classroom wrapped around Brianne Somersby. Stupid, fake, tall, silky-haired and skinny-legged Brianne.

I wanted to be the wronged romance heroine then, fortified with elegance and resolve. I wanted to act strong, brave, and unharmed in the face of this treachery. Planning my escape, I took a deep, bracing breath. Which somehow got caught in my throat and made me choke. Which made me cough. Which made me cry. Not a gentle, heartbroken sob, or a petite sniffle. More like the roar of a wounded lioness.

Somehow my howl was enough to break Jesse and Brianne out of their embrace. Not to mention effectively stopping all traffic in the hallway. With most of the student body staring at me, I decided it was my cue to speak.

"Jesse, are . . . ?" Okay, that wasn't quite it.

"How?" Maybe I wasn't making myself clear.

"Why?" And we had communication. If I was expecting a guilty look, I had another disappointment coming.

"Hey, Sarah. What's up?" He smirked, his arm sliding

easily behind Brianne's back. At least she had the decency to look ashamed. Or maybe she was just embarrassed that the whole school knew she was making out in front of the Spanish classroom.

"What are you doing?" I shouted into his face. With all the benefits of hindsight, this stands out as the dumbest part.

He actually looked around, taking stock of his audience. His arm still held Brianne in clutch, and that stupid smirk on his face made his dimples deepen—those ridiculous dimples that up to that moment had seemed so adorable.

"I'm getting ready for my Spanish test. Good-luck charm," he said, nodding at Brianne.

Struggling with my horror and confusion, I had a second to wonder if Brianne objected to his condescending tone. Shaking my head, I spluttered, "But you . . . we're supposed to be . . . I thought . . . I mean . . . Jesse, what about me?"

If I thought the hallway was quiet before, it was nothing compared to the absolute silence that fell now. I could feel the air stagnate as the senior class waited to breathe.

And then he laughed. It was the ugliest, most hateful sound I'd ever heard. "Oh, come on." He spoke not to me, but to his audience in the hall. "What? You think we're dating or some-thing? Give me a break." That horrible laugh again. "Like I'd be dating the fat girl when I could have *this*." And he gestured to Brianne's lip-gloss-and-highlights perfection.

Turning to run, I smacked right into McCall. She could have been Jesse's twin, with that smirk and those dimples. She put her face right up to mine and whispered, "Told you."

I knew she was right. It all clicked into place then, as I el-bowed my way through the laughing crowd to the parking lot: our "first date" to translate that paragraph for his Spanish class, our "dates" over his stupid geometry proofs, holding hands on his parents' couch while we watched a black-and-white version of *King Lear* so I could help him write a paper on a play he couldn't be bothered to read. I had been tricked. Double-crossed. Deceived. Defrauded. Swindled. By the king of the outlaws, no less. Jesse Chandler became Jesse James that very afternoon.

Now, in the corner by the vending machine, I can't think straight. I'm drowning under my past humiliation and the current scrutiny.

Shari can see it and she throws me a line. "Sorry I'm going to be gone so I can't see you play the party with your boyfriend. What about you guys—are you in?" She's all business, but she just has to slip in that part about boyfriends.

"I'll come watch you and your boyfriend. Can I bring a date?" Dean asks.

"Sure, of course," I tell him, surprised and relieved. As long as his date isn't the Boss. The thought almost makes me smile, and I relax for the first time in this conversation.

Tandy looks at Maura and nods. "We'll be there," Maura says.

"Thanks, guys. You're the best proofreader cubicle buddies a girl could ask for."

"You mean a *girlfriend* could ask for," Dean smirks.

I decide to let that go. This time.

⌒⌒

With a week and a half until the long Thanksgiving weekend, all the professors seem to be turning up the heat. There are papers due all over the place. Dr. Younger, who is way too nice to be related to the outlaws who ran with the James brothers, has still not grabbed a clue about Krissy. He continues to let her speak in class.

"I was riding a white horse through the Library at Alexandria," she murmurs. "Scrolls were flying at my horse's feet. The Universe is advising me to storm the knowledge of the ages."

It's a classic bimbo line, delivered with the perfect amount of breathiness. It's so excellent that I'm actually trying not to giggle, and I'm not even a giggler. I put my head on my desk to stop from shaking. I sneak a glance up at Dr. Younger, who is nodding his head as if in agreement.

He says, "Well, that's lucky for you. You're in the right place."

*I wish I could tell Ben.*

*Not a chance.*

*I know, but it's so funny. He'd crack up.*

*He'd never laugh if he knew it was his cousin we were mocking.*

*Yeah, probably. No, wait. He might. Because it's that funny, no matter who you're related to.*

*Don't risk it.*

*Don't worry. I'll just add it to my list of things to wish.*

Chirp. A text arrives. It's from Ben.

R U BIZY THANKSGVG?

It's funny how, now, even his misspelled texts make me shudder a little thinking about learning disabilities.

NO BIG PLANS THURS, I reply. Maybe he's forgotten our

horrifying little commitment for Friday night. I'm not about to remind him.

WIL U CME FR DINR?

What does that mean? Like to his home? His parents' home for a holiday dinner? That sounds like a girlfriend thing to do. I can feel myself hyperventilating. Little black spots start dancing in front of my eyes.

PLEEZ. PLEEZ. PLEEZ. WNT U THER.

An unanticipated shiver of what is either horror or delight runs through me, and I can feel electricity in my scalp, curling my hair (as if it needed the help).

*What's the hold-up, sister?*

*I don't know what to say.*

*Yes, you do. You say yes. You want to go, so say yes.*

*Okay, but it's scary.*

*No, it's not. You just punch in the following message: Y-E-S. Very simple.*

*But why?*

*Because it's rude to leave him hanging. You need to answer him.*

*No, I mean why does he want me there?*

*Are we still having this conversation? You're an idiot. Who cares why he wants you there? He wants you there. Just say yes.*

*Yes?*

*Yes.*

YES.

YES? YAY!

LOVE 2 COME. WHAT TIME? WHAT CAN I BRING? See how my mother raised me right?

DINR @ 4, BUT CM ALL DAY. I'L PICK U UP. MOM SEZ BRING POTATS IF U CN HANDL IT.

If I can handle it? Ha. I'll show them potatoes.

# Chapter Thirteen

It's cold outside. Ben drives me home from Caleb's after study group, and I wonder if he's going to come in to practice playing for the party. Or come in for any other reason. He's been acting a little weird tonight. He didn't say anything during study group. He just sat at the table and stared at his hands. He's still pretty quiet, so naturally I get uncomfortable.

"Hey, you okay?" I ask in a really casual way, which implies that I know he's perfectly fine, but shows that I'm sensitive.

He nods.

I'm glad we're almost to my apartment. I hate driving in silence. And his ancient car doesn't have a functional radio.

He pulls into an empty parking spot and looks over at me. I am surprised to see how sad he looks. If I looked that sad, I'd be crying. I want to reach over and give him a hug, but then I'd look like some sort of hussy. So I settle for being forward in a safer way.

"Want to come up for a while? We should practice."

He just nods again, and I try to remember if I've actually

heard him speak at all today. I know he said he'd pick me up for study group, so if it's laryngitis, it came on sometime after lunch. I jump out of the car and walk toward the door. He grabs his guitar out of the backseat and follows me up the stairs. I know we're in for trouble when I see flickering light through the slats in the blinds. Candles. That means Mandy's home.

I take a deep breath and open the door, preparing to block whatever scene of terror masquerading as romance that Mandy and her guy have going on. The smell of incense mixes with Mandy's hiccupping, and the coffee table is hidden under a mountain of tissues.

Lauren is sitting on the arm of the couch with Mandy's head on her leg. She looks up in alarm, but relaxes her face when she sees Ben and me.

"Oh, it's just you. Good. Shut the door. Don't let the healing essence out. We need it here."

I have no idea what to do with the situation before me. Ben is moping, Mandy is sobbing, and Lauren is speaking more words than I've ever heard from her at one time. Closing the door, I nod Ben toward the kitchen. He walks off, slumping and slow.

I kneel on the floor in front of Mandy. Her eyes, red and swollen, blink up at me from behind her hair.

"We broke up," she stutters.

I hate that. Couldn't she be more specific? Does that mean he dumped her and she accepts it? Or she ended it and she regrets it? Or did they somehow stop kissing long enough to come to a mutual decision? Since I don't know how it happened, it's hard to know what tone to take. If I say that I'm sorry, I'll be lying. Because why would I be sorry to have him out of the apartment? Instead I reach out and stroke her hand.

"He likes someone else," she says in a flat voice between sobs. "But I will never, ever care for anyone else." Sob. "He was everything to me and now I have nothing."

I would love to be the kind of person who can give positive, uplifting, greeting-card-style words of encouragement at times like this, but all that's coming to me is "Get over it." I decide to keep my mouth shut. It's not like she's just lost a real romance hero. The guy was a nothing. But she doesn't seem to think so. She's acting like he was the greatest man in the world.

Mandy sits up, wipes her eyes, blows her nose, and shakes her hair out of her face. Lauren's been rubbing circles on her back, but stands now.

"I'll run you a bath," she says, picking up the incense and a candle and heading off down the hall. We hear the water start, and Mandy looks apologetic.

"Sorry about the mess," she says, taking in the room that's knee-deep in quilted two-ply.

"No problem. I'll get it. Just go relax for a while." I don't say any of the things I'm thinking about her needing to come to her senses or realizing she's better off or knowing it was wrong from the start.

She smiles at me, the saddest face full of heartache and misery and fear. She really thinks this is the end of her world. As I give her an awkward little hug, I realize that I don't know this girl at all.

Sweeping the tissues into the garbage can in the living room proves to be a futile exercise. I grab a trash bag from the kitchen, telling Ben I'll be right back. I try not to think about what I'm touching as I load up a roomful of used tissues. Tying off the bag I head back to the kitchen to find Ben sitting at the table with his head on his arm.

"I'm so sorry about that. Minor heartbreak emergency. It's a girl thing," I say as I wash my hands in the sink.

He almost laughs, but it sounds more like a sigh.

"Um, are you all right?"

"I'm a little tired."

"Oh, do you want to go home?"

"No, Sarah, I mean I'm tired of this. Of working so hard."

I look around the room. What is he working so hard about? He's sitting at the table. He's not even studying.

He takes a breath, like he needs to buck up for something. "You are making me tired. My heart is tired."

That seems like a strange thing to say. I want to say something back, but I don't feel quite into this conversation yet. My head is full of Mandy's imagined tragedy and I have no frame of reference for Ben now.

"I can never tell what you're thinking. I know I'm not smart enough to read you. Maybe I have to ask really simple questions."

I watch him. I don't know what I'm thinking either, so I wait for him to go on.

Now his voice is quiet, almost a whisper. "Are you interested in me at all? In us? Because if you are, you're sure good at hiding it."

It feels like the air leaves the room. My heart beats one loud thud in my ears. Why would he ask me that? Of course I'm interested in him. What does he mean that I'm hiding it?

He looks strange. His eyebrows are squished together and his face is turning red. His voice is still quiet and sad. "You have never called me, not once. You have never shown up at my place. You have never asked me over if I didn't invite myself first. You've never even taken my hand. You've never kissed me first. I'm putting myself out there now, because I'm totally crazy about you. But if this comes as a surprise to you, maybe you need to tell me so. I think I've been pretty plain, but I know I'm not as smart as you are. Or as smart as anyone. I didn't think that mattered to you so much, but I guess it does. There's nothing else I can really do about it. I don't want to play games, and . . . You know what? I think I just need to leave you alone for a while."

He gets up from the chair and, without looking at me, walks straight out the door. He is gone, and I don't say a thing to stop him.

I have no idea what just happened.

In a Whirl is crowded and noisy, filled with people rushing around wearing coats and eating warm pastry and being excited that a holiday is coming. Chel holds my hand and picks at her muffin. And I try to explain.

"It's not a fight. You know me, I don't fight. He didn't get mad, or yell, or tell me off. He just sounded sad and hurt and . . . like a guy with a broken heart. What am I doing?"

"It sounds like you broke up with him."

"But I didn't even speak. I didn't say a word," I whine, close to tears now.

"Not even a word like *no* or *please* or *stay?*"

Well, when she puts it like that, it does sort of sound like I broke up with him. We keep using that phrase, but how could we break up when we were just friends, anyway?

*Just friends who kiss?*

*Hey, you, butt out.*

*I'm just saying that maybe it's time you recognize something, here.*

*Fine, I'm open to revelations. What?*

*Ben was your boyfriend and you let him slide away.*

*But, I—*

*He spent all his time with you.*

*Yeah, but—*

*You never saw him with another girl.*

*Okay, but—*

*He called, he texted, he came over, he hugged, he kissed, he flirted, he ate, he praised—he Sought You Out.*

*(!)*

*Well, there you go.*

*He did, didn't he? He really did. I was being Sought, just like a real romance heroine. Just like I've always wanted to be. And the whole time it was happening, I was missing it. I missed it because I didn't believe it could be happening, not to me. Even while he was Seeking, I was looking over my shoulder, waiting for the inevitable ending where he finds his real match, his soul mate, his princess.*

I grab the crunchy paper napkins on the table and try to hide the fact that my guilt is falling out of my eyes and all down my face.

"I really screwed this up, didn't I?"

"Yeah, sweetie, you did. But you can fix it. And I hope you will. Quickly. So your heart will be happy, and his heart will be happy, and so my party will still rock." She smiles.

"What do I do now?" I ask her.

She digs my phone out of my bag and hands it to me. Then she pops out of the booth and pushes her way through the crowds to flirt with Zak. She's just making everyone feel better today.

Holding the phone, I realize that what Ben said last night is true. I have never called him. I never wanted to be so forward. I have never even called him back. My fingers have never dialed his number. I scroll down to the Bs and find him, but I just stare at the screen full of his number. What do I say? What will he say? How do I maintain any kind of personal dignity?

*Is that what you're after, here? Personal dignity?*

*Well, among other things.*

*Let it go. Just make the call.*

My finger moves closer to the button, but I can't make it connect. Closer again, then back. It's like a pair of magnets turned the wrong way—there's an undeniable force pushing my finger away from the "call" button. I set the phone on the table, take a deep breath, shake out my shoulders, and try again.

*It's not that hard. Just push the button. The little green one, right there. You'll be so glad you did it.*

*I'm working on it.*

*Almost there . . . just touch it.*

*Go easy on me, here. I'm trying.*

*WILL YOU PUSH THE BUTTON?*

I close my eyes, breathe in all the good vibes of the busy smoothie shop, and punch the button. The hang-up button.

All the bones in my back go limp and I slump over the table. I am defeated by my own idiocy. I'd sort of like to cry now, but suddenly I feel too tired. I'll just stay here with my hair in my muffin crumbs and work hard to breathe—in and out, in and out. Chel's bound to notice me sooner or later, and when she does, she'll come get me. She'll help me sit up straight again. She'll probably even pick the crumbs out of my curls.

But it isn't Chel who comes. It's Zak. I can feel him fold himself onto the bench across from me and slide the crumby plate out from under my hair. Then he moves my smoothie out of my reach in case I go nuts and either chuck it at him or fling my arms in despair. Even though he's wearing a very masculine apron, he probably doesn't want my drink all down his front.

He pats my hair. Not in any romantic way, not even in a particularly comforting way. Just patting, in rhythm. Almost drumming. For several long minutes.

I raise my head a little, so my chin rests on the table, instead of my forehead. His face is inches away from mine, his chin in his hand, his arm on the table. His other hand is still in my hair. He has his eyebrows raised, as if to ask what's going on, and it is all suddenly so ridiculous. Him, sitting across the table from me, drumming on my head, while I sprawl limp and boneless across a mess of streusel topping. Nothing is fixed, and maybe nothing will ever be fixed, but right now, life is just too funny. I sit up, grab Zak's drumming fingers in both my hands and laugh. He looks a little startled, but he laughs with me. He reaches down and adds his other hand to the mix, and we sit there in the window of In a Whirl, holding hands and laughing.

I believe I may be in an early state of shock.

Do I care? Not so much. It feels so good to laugh that I keep doing it. My shoulders are shaking, my hands clench Zak's fingers, my cheeks start to ache. And this is the moment I choose to look out the window.

And see Ben.

Standing on the sidewalk, a little disheveled, staring at us through the window and looking sad. As soon as our eyes meet, he turns and walks away—very fast. I couldn't catch him if I tried. So I don't even get out of the seat. Because I can't. I am trapped in the booth by the realization of what has just happened.

I have lived a moment out of a romance novel.

*But it was completely the wrong moment.*

Why? Why do I get to live the "misunderstanding moment"? Why does the hero of my story have to catch me in what looks like a compromising situation with another guy? Why did he have to see me holding hands and laughing with very cute Zak?

"Um, Sarah? You're kind of scaring me." Zak looks confused and worried. "I was okay with the passed-out Sarah on the table, and I was really good with the hysterical Sarah. But the Sarah who looks like she's going to hurl—I'm not so sure."

Shaking my head, I point out the window at the spot where Ben's back disappeared.

"What? That was him?"

I nod.

"And he saw you? Us?"

Another nod.

"And it looked a little bit like we were having a thing, didn't it?"

Holding my head to avoid another tabletop collapse, I nod again.

He pushes my head up with his finger so I can see his face. "Is he going to beat me up?" Zak whispers.

I can't help it. I laugh again. And start to cry. I wish I could throw up. I want my mommy. But I know that talking to my mom wouldn't help at all, so I put my head back down on the table and try to forget.

## Chapter Fourteen

I sit in my usual place in Novetsky's theater. If he doesn't come sit by me, I'll find him after class. I will. I will walk up to him and tell him there was a mistake. Or two. And that we need to talk it out. And that everything can be the same, because everything *is* the same. Nothing has changed. We are still good. And still friends. Still good friends.

He doesn't come. Caleb takes the empty seat beside me a minute after class starts. The quiz is half over when I hear the door open and close. I just about give myself whiplash looking for Ben, but it is a girl who came in late.

When the lecture starts, I can't concentrate. I look back at the door so often that I must be creating a breeze with my hair flying back and forth. I half-listen to Novetsky say that she's going to be reading some of our papers aloud over the next few classes, but the words barely register. At the end of the lecture, I look one more time at the door, but there's no Ben.

As I shove my computer into my bag, I feel a hand on my shoulder. Electricity runs down my arm, straight into my stomach, and out the ends of my hair. He's here? He found me? He got my two really lame-but-brave phone messages from Sunday? I put on my happy smile and look up. Right into the deep chocolate eyes of the godlike TA. I had already started to stand, so I have to go through with it. He leans with his arm on the back of my chair, looking at me and smiling back.

"Sarah, right?"

Holy cow. He speaks my name.

I nod, trying to keep my face from betraying my panic.

"So Professor Novetsky liked your paper, and she wants to read it in class."

I stare dumbly. He must think I can't hear him over the noise of the emptying theater because he leans in closer (closer!) and says it again.

*Get a grip. He's not hitting on you. He just wants your permission to have your paper read.*

*I know. But he's standing so close.*

*Shake it off and answer him. Politely.*

"Okay. Sure. That sounds great. When?" I manage to get all these words out without squeaking or shouting or falling over. Then I glance past his shoulder.

No way. The Universe is not so cruel.

This is not happening.

What did he just hear me say?

Ben is standing behind the godlike TA in a little crowd of people trying to leave the room. He must have been sitting at the front of the hall. I didn't see him because he was already there when I showed up. Maybe he was waiting for me to find him.

I can feel the heat behind my eyeballs. Did Ben hear me talk to this guy? Did it sound like what it was, or did it sound like what it wasn't? I try to catch his eye, but he's looking at the floor, brushing past the TA to leave the room.

"Ben," I call, but he doesn't turn. Maybe he can't hear me. I want to run after him, but I can't. Besides not being that kind of a girl, I'm wedged between Caleb and a really handsome but totally inconvenient TA.

The TA who is still standing here.

"Okay, well, good job on your paper."

"Mm-hmm. Thanks," I manage.

Ben is very, very gone. I slump off toward philosophy, already dreading the freakish tangents that may well come up during the lecture. Then I think of Miss Existential Journey Girl and a new horror is added to the usual.

What if she knows something?

*Oh, come on. What could she know?*

*Something. Anything. What if she talked to him and she knows?*

*Who cares? It's not like she'll talk to you. Forget about it. It's fine.*

Well, not so fine. As I walk in the room, she's standing by the door. Watching me with eyes squinted almost shut, she turns and walks beside me as I pass. She follows me to my seat and sits. Not next to me, not behind me, but *on my desk*. Surprise rattles my brain and I can't even tell her to take off. I just look at her and wait. Is she about to break the silent treatment?

"Happy now?" she asks.

Grateful that she's being quiet about it, but not grateful enough to be nice, I shoot back, "Happy that you're sitting on my desk? Not particularly."

"I mean, are you happy you broke his heart? Happy that you wrecked him?"

I'm not at all sure what to say. Obviously they've talked about this whatever-it-is. But I don't know how to use this to my advantage. Should I buddy up to her and get the dirt? Can she give me information that will help me get back in Ben's good graces?

I take a breath and prepare to be mature. I'm nearly ready to ask the wise questions that will reveal to me the mysteries of my life that apparently this girl already knows.

But she won't wait for me. "You don't even care, do you? You stomp on his feelings and then run around flirting and going out with other guys." She says it like it's the worst thing ever, and like it's true. Her scornful face is much too close to mine.

Okay. The gloves are coming off. Why should I pretend to be nice to her, anyway? "You have no idea what you're talking about. If this were any of your business—which it isn't—I might tell you that you have got it totally wrong. I'm not going out with other guys. Even if anyone asked, which no one did."

"But he saw you. Holding hands with some guy in that smoothie place. And he just heard someone else in your art class ask you out."

Wow. She works fast. That couldn't have happened more than seven minutes ago.

"You think you're going to play all these different guys, but Ben's not going to be one of them. Not now that he knows what kind of person you really are." She says all this with a venomous hiss in her voice, and I realize that she hates me.

Has that ever happened before? I mean, yeah, I decided weeks ago that I hated her, but now *she* hates *me*. I don't think I've ever known anyone who hates me before. Not that everyone likes me—of course not. Most people in the world, and even in my general vicinity, don't even know I'm alive. I've never had anyone look at me like the way she is looking at me. She wants to hit me. She wants to hurt me. It's very hot in here, and I'm a little scared.

"You think he's stupid, but he's not. He's smart enough to know that you're all wrong for him. He doesn't need you to make him feel dumb."

Dr. Younger calls the class to order and Krissy slips off my desk. I'm hoping she'll take a seat far away, or—even better—decide that she's too upset to stay in class. But she not only takes the seat right beside me, she shoves her chair closer to me. She stares at the side of my face, shooting spears with her eyes.

Wow. She really loves Ben.

*Or she really hates me.*

*Well, why else would she feel that way? She thinks you're hurting him, and she wants to protect him.*

*Don't you dare defend her. She's insane.*

I want to try calling him again, but obviously not now. Maybe I can send him a quick text. I pull out my phone and scroll to his number. Out of the corner of my eye I can see her, still staring me down. Hands under the desk, I thumb a message.

HI. CAN WE TALK? PLS CALL.—S

I want to keep the phone out so I'll get his reply as soon as he sends it, but I saw Dr. Younger bust a guy last week for texting. How embarrassing. I shove my phone into my bag and glance over at Krissy again. She must have seen me send the text, because she now looks not only angry but also disgusted. She disapproves of my motives, whatever she thinks they are.

Dr. Younger blasts a quiz up on the screen. I read the

questions, but all the answers seem ridiculous. They're all the same. Okay, I know they're not, but the differences are so picky.

> According to Socrates, all people are seeking
> 1. pleasure.
> 2. what is in their self-interest.
> 3. to help others as much as possible.
> 4. rightly or wrongly to do their duty.
> 5. what is serviceable to society.

*What am I seeking?*

> According to Socrates, if a person is ignorant, then that person
> 1. will make wrong decisions.
> 2. will make bad decisions.
> 3. will not make good decisions.
> 4. is what others call "evil."
> 5. is all of the above.

*How ignorant do I have to be to have landed myself—and Ben—in this stupid mess?*

> According to Socrates, sometimes we make good decisions when we
> 1. act rightly.
> 2. act on the basis of our knowledge.
> 3. are not ignorant of the relevant facts.
> 4. are correctly informed and knowledgeable.
> 5. are all of the above.

*Can I even remember my last good decision when it comes to Ben?*

> The most important thing in living a life of
> excellence is, according to Socrates,
>> 1. to do only that which we know to be right.
>> 2. to survive and prosper.
>> 3. to seek pleasure and avoid pain.
>> 4. to distinguish between things in our control and
>> things outside our control.
>> 5. none of the above.

*Is my life excellent? Am I right? Am I surviving and prospering? Is this pleasure or pain? Is there actually anything in my control?*

*Not so much. None of the above.*

I drag myself into the proofreading cube ten minutes late. This is a first, and I know someone's going to give me a hard time about it. I manage to avoid the Boss, but Maura, Tandy, Shari, and Dean are all looking at me and smiling when I walk in. Maura is actually rubbing her black-nailed hands together in anticipation.

"So, how was your weekend?" Maura asks, wiggling her eyebrows.

"Ugh," is all I can manage. This seems to surprise them.

"What went wrong?" Shari is quick to the point.

"Chronologically or alphabetically?" I don't wait for an answer, because I'm a little afraid they'll actually make me alphabetize this stupid weekend. "Friday's study group was a washout, Ben was acting like a silent movie, Make-Out Mandy got dumped and we were swimming in wadded up tissue, and somehow, Ben and I fell apart. Saturday he may or may not have seen me holding hands and laughing with someone who may or may not be really cute and male. And he also refused to answer my calls—Ben, not the other guy. Also the next day he wouldn't answer the phone, although I have never actually called him on a Sunday before, so maybe his phone takes a day of rest." Nobody laughs, which is just as well. It isn't funny.

"And yesterday he heard something that sounded strangely, impossibly, like me making a date with the art history TA."

All three girls stare, openmouthed. See? He's famous. "Don't worry. It was totally misinterpreted. The TA just wanted to read my paper during class, and I said okay. But he's kind of beautiful, and he was standing really close, and I was just a little bit . . . enchanted."

Dean shakes his head in disgust. I can't blame him. Not at all.

Shari asks, "So what happened Friday, with Ben?"

Do they really need to hear this? Guilty and humiliated, I tell them. "Apparently I haven't been acting exactly like the you-know-what."

Blank stares.

"You know."

Head shakes.

I do a huffy breath of impatience. "Like the *girlfriend*," I confess.

Ah, the I-told-you-so face. Yeah, that. Times four.

"Wow. Sorry about that. Need some chocolate?" Tandy offers.

I shake my head. Chocolate is not going to help, unless it's in ice cream.

Dean, all business, says, "Well, now you know. Next time you won't be such a jerk, and things will work out better." He turns back to his monitor.

Maura is indignant for me. "Thanks, Dear Abby. What do you know about it, anyway?"

Shari pipes in with one of her gems of creative grammar. "Hey, Dean. Get some nice."

His face shows his surprise. "Look around the cubicle, ladies. This isn't about being nice. This is about being realistic. None of you has been on my end of this kind of thing before. I'm a guy, remember?"

"Okay, let me have it," I say, resigned.

"Let's just say you're a beautiful girl, willing to play the game with a guy. Like chess."

Chess? I'm totally ready to interrupt and change his story to reflect reality, but he's stunned me a little with the "beautiful" part.

"So he moves a piece—say, a pawn—and you let him. He waits for a minute, and you don't move. So he moves again. And waits. Then he makes another little move, and you let him. Are you seeing a pattern here? I'm just saying, sooner or later, he's got to wonder why he's the only one doing anything. And he's got to figure that it's because you're just killing time. So he backs off to give you a chance to play the game, but you refuse. He figures that either you don't want to play the game, or you don't want to play it with him. So he ducks out. If, let's just say hypothetically, he then sees you playing the game with someone else, he's going to quit. It's not that complicated."

He leans back in his roller chair with his hands behind his

head as casual as if he has not just dropped a huge revelation in my lap. Still stunned, I walk behind him, take his face in my hands, and plant a kiss on the top of his head.

He looks around very obviously, pretending to hide behind the cubicle wall. Yeah, yeah. I get it. If Ben saw that, we'd all just die a humiliated death.

I sit down again in my chair. "Thank you for clearing up my life's mess, you keeper of masculine wisdom. You know that if you weren't here, we would have talked in circles all afternoon, eaten pounds of chocolate, and left feeling worse. So can you tell me what I should do now?"

"I guess you already know. It's your move."

"But he won't answer the phone," I whine. Am I ever going to stop doing that?

Dean shakes his head. "He may not be answering, but he knows you're calling. Try again. The way it looks from here, you're a few turns behind." He turns back to his computer and starts typing just as the Boss puts her head around the corner.

"How are we doing on the spring term courses? I need to see them all proofed by the first week in December."

We nod together, and she retreats to whatever it is she does on her side of the wall. Tandy pulls a whiteboard marker out of her drawer, points to where the Boss just left, and pretends to inhale the marker fumes. It feels great to laugh, even silently.

As I leave work I take a moment to enjoy the strangely warm afternoon in all its golden fall light. The leaves catch the sun, the breeze is gentle, and I'm feeling altogether more brave than usual. I take a deep breath and push the call button. The message box doesn't pick up immediately. I take this as a good sign—at least his phone is on. I let my breathing follow the rings. In, out. In, out. He's not going to answer. In, out.

"Hello?"

I gasp in a breath, and naturally manage to choke on it. Coughing, I hold the phone away from my head for a second.

*Come on, Sarah. Get in control.*

*I can't breathe.*

*Try.*

"Sorry," I squeak between coughs and gasps. I can feel tears in the corners of my eyes. I am the world's biggest idiot. Getting it together, I manage to inhale without exploding.

"Are you sick?"

Does he sound hopeful?

"No, I'm good. Just a little . . . I don't know what. Um, how are you?"

"Fine."

Well. We're not winning any communications awards today.

"Are you on campus?"

"Just leaving the library," he says.

"Do you have a minute? Want to meet me?" This feels so strange. What happened to the comfortable, the familiar?

*You let it walk away, remember?*

*Oh. Right.*

I can hear him breathing. Why is it taking him so long to say he wants to meet me?

Because he doesn't? Or maybe because it's my turn to meet him?

I turn around on the sidewalk, still listening to him breathe into the phone. Heading toward the library, I decide to be brave. "Ben, I hate this. Can we please fix it? I . . ."—can I say it?—"I miss . . . I miss having you around." It comes out quieter than I'd planned. I hope he heard me, because I doubt I could ever say that again.

I walk fast, scanning the crowds near the library. I hear him say, "I miss being around."

I see him. He's sitting with his back against the west wall of the library, his head tipped back and his elbows on his knees. In a romance novel, this would be the part right after the hero ranted around, tearing at his hair and throwing furniture. The slightly pathetic letdown time that, come to think of it, probably wouldn't make it into the book at all. And maybe it's time for me to put the stupid book down, now. I'm close enough to see that his eyes are closed, and he hasn't noticed me.

About twenty feet away from him, I sit down against the building too. I can watch him decide if he ever wants to talk to me again.

"So are you heading somewhere?" I'm such a cheater. What if he lies? Could I escape before he sees me here?

"No. I'll go home later."

"Do you want to talk to me?" Do I sound confident? Aggressive? Desperate?

There is enough of a pause here for me to feel completely ridiculous. Was it really such a hard question?

"Yeah. I want to talk to you. I want to tell you something. I figured something out. I miss you. I miss being around you. And I want to be your friend, if that's what you want."

Relief rolls over me. If that's what I want? "Of course I want that." It feels so good to be in agreement again. This is great.

I watch as his head slides off the library wall and down into his hand. What did I say? He looks wrecked. Didn't I just agree with him? We want to be friends. That's good, right? Great, even. So why does that make him look so sad? Maybe that's not a sad posture. Maybe that's how he looks when he's relieved.

"Great. That's great." His cheerful voice doesn't match his

slouch against the wall, but I'm going to believe it. "Where are you? Leaving work?"

I jump up from the ground and hustle back around the corner. "Actually I was coming to find you. I'm almost at the library." True.

"I'll meet you by the back door," he says, and I see him stand up, close his phone, and brush off his pants. Following him, I see him straighten as he walks toward the door. He rolls his shoulders like in a warm-up exercise.

I feel such relief that we're back in my zone, in the place where I feel like I belong. No, not the library, but the place where I want to be with him and he wants to be with me and we're not pretending to be anything weird. Just friends. I won't need to pretend to be the girl I'm not, and he won't need to pretend that I am either. No more stupid fantasies that only happen in dumb books. I count to ten and walk around the corner to the door.

*Wow. I almost forgot how perfect he is.*

*What was that bit about feeling all comfortable and relaxed?*

*Yeah, forget that part. I'm a wreck. He's too beautiful.*

*So what? Can't a great-looking guy hang out with anyone he wants to?*

*Yeah, I guess. But doesn't it make you wonder about his sanity, just a little?*

*That's a pretty sane smile.*

True. He looks happy to see me. And I am thrilled to look at his great face. I wave, and he takes a step toward me. Then he stops, so I move my pawn. Dean would be so proud. I walk right up to him and give him a hug. Like any friend would. He leans his head into my hair, and I can feel him breathing. I command my knees to remain strong.

"Are you hungry?" I ask him. "Let's go get a snack. On me—I just got paid." Lie. But convincing enough. And sort of like moving another pawn.

The smell of greasy food draws us to the corner on the edge of campus. I order two cheeseburgers and a huge basket of fries and wait at the counter while Ben finds a seat. It's not hard—it's only 4:30—but apparently eating here is always a good idea because there are quite a few people. Is he going to be embarrassed if someone he knows sees us together? But really, why should he be? We are friends. Friends can eat together.

I slide into the booth across from him and toss him a burger. Mine tastes excellent. There's something about onions melted into processed cheese products. He doesn't say much while we eat, and that's fine. What needs to be said, anyway?

"So about this weekend," he says as he plays with a fry.

Oh. Right. That may need to be said.

"Are you still up for coming to my house for Thanksgiving dinner?"

I don't even try to hide how pleased I am. I can feel a big smile cross my face, and I don't even worry if there's food in my teeth. I swallow before I ask, "Am I still invited?"

"Sure." He shrugs. "If you want to come. I mean, you have to eat somewhere, right?"

He's sounding awkward again. Maybe he doesn't want people around us to hear that he has plans with me. I lower my voice and say, "I'd really love to spend the day with you."

He looks up from the mutilated fry in his hands and smiles, just enough so that his one forward tooth pokes out a tiny bit.

"And Chel's party?" he asks.

"What do you think?" I'm reverting to my backward ways. "Do you still want to do it?"

He looks down again. "We said we would. We sort of committed. She's counting on us. I think it's only fair to her if we still play. Even if it means we have to do something we're not really looking forward to."

Ouch. We are not really back to good here. He's being too careful. Does he not want to? Or does he think I don't want to?

# *Chapter Fifteen*

Happy Thanksgiving, dear. We're so glad you could come." Ben's mom looks like she's about to cry. Yeah, so glad I could come. "Please excuse me. I've got to get back to the kitchen."

Something is weird here. It's different than the wedding reception day. Everyone is being fairly polite, but nobody seems happy to see me. Ben's dad shakes my hand and then sits down with a newspaper. The siblings are all watching me as though I'm some kind of dangerous. They'll make eye contact if I stare directly at them, but only for a second. Except for Megan, the newly married sister. She can't seem to look at me at all. And it's not like she's totally absorbed in her amazing husband. True, she's always touching him, but she's still looking around, talking with her brothers and sisters. Just not with me.

Can Ben even see how uncomfortable this is, sitting around the living room with people who wish I wasn't there? Maybe I should say something. But what would I say?

Hey, Ben, why does everyone here think I should go home now? And should I?

Since your family hates me, how about we wait out dinner in some less crowded part of the house?

Oh, I have an idea. How about I leave the bowl of mashed potatoes and go home to my empty apartment?

I'd like to take a walk now—and never come back.

"I'm going to check on the kids. Want to come?" Ben asks. I don't know if he's being chivalrous, or if he really thinks there's any chance I'd like to stay, unprotected, in the midst of his family. But I nod and we walk down to the basement, where a bunch of little people jump on and hang off various pieces of furniture. One girl who looks about three years old leaps off the couch and into Ben's arms. She holds his face between her hands and rubs his nose with hers.

I want to do that.

*Don't you dare.*

*Of course I'm not going to. But you have to admit, it looks like a good idea.*

Standing against the wall, I watch Uncle Ben become the new favorite piece of furniture. The kids jump on him and tackle him and roll around with him. He's so great with them. One girl who looks like the oldest walks over and leans next to me against the wall.

"Hello, Sarah." She's so formal and serious. And she must be related to the lot upstairs, because she's not making eye contact either.

"Hi. We met at Megan's reception, didn't we?" I stab.

Now she looks. With disdain. I didn't know that look could fit a face that young. "No. I live in Minnesota. We couldn't come for both the wedding and the holiday, so we had to pick one. We're just here for the weekend." She shakes her head as though she could erase my stupid image from the Etch-a-Sketch that is her brain.

"Oh. Well, welcome, I guess. What's your name?"

"Raquel. With a Q-U. I'm seven."

(Note to self: Want a drama queen? Give a kid a name with a "q-u" in it.)

"Well, Raquel, I'm very glad to meet you. Thanks for coming over to talk to me."

She shrugs. "You don't have any friends here."

I stare at the side of her head as she watches her cousins play.

*She couldn't have meant that the way it sounded.*

*Except, she could have. What a little witch.*

*No, she's just being . . . something.*

*Brutally honest?*

"Except Uncle Ben, I guess," she continues. "Everyone knows you want to be his friend."

Who is everyone? What is she talking about? Have these people been discussing how I've been chasing Ben around? Oh, that's lovely. They've obviously been discussing something. Maybe someone should teach them not to gossip in front of little kids.

Or maybe I can use this to my advantage.

"I don't have any friends here, either, you know." Her voice is almost inaudible.

Recovering almost quickly enough to hide my awkward surprise, I ask, "What about all these cousins?"

"They're all too little. I'm the oldest. And I don't live here. Except for on vacations. Then I have my own room. Want to see it?"

"I'd love to see your room." And just that fast, she changes from a small, witchy person to a cute little girl.

She takes my hand and leads me up the stairs. We pass the hallway leading to the living room, where all the other adults are making unstrained and friendly conversation now that I'm not there. There's still something strange about the house today, though. I can't figure out what it is.

Raquel opens a door with pink stars painted on it and shows me into her room. There's a little white daybed (made neatly with no sheets poking out) and two dressers with mirrors. Along the opposite wall, there's a huge desk surrounded by filing cabinets. She sees me looking, and says, "I let my grandma share my room when I'm not here. She uses it for an office."

"That's very nice of you. Do your mom and dad share this room with you, too?"

Here's that look again. The one that says so clearly, *Poor Sarah, you're so dumb.* "No. They have their own room on the other side of Uncle Ben's."

Intriguing piece of information. I point to the wall. "Is that Uncle Ben's room?"

Nodding, she tells me about their schemes. "He wants to put a hole in the wall so we can pass messages. He said he'd hide the hole behind a picture of me. And also, if I lay on the floor right here, I can talk to him through the heater. And he's teaching me that tap-tap code, you know?"

"Morse code? Really?" I don't want to laugh at her, because she's absolutely right about me not having any friends here. I can't afford to offend the only person who will speak to me.

She nods. "I read about it in a story, and he said he'll teach it to me."

"I think that's very cool."

She gives me the first smile that looks like it belongs on a little girl. "Do you want to see Uncle Ben's room?"

Do I ever. But I know that at this point, any wrong move I make is going to be witnessed by at least a dozen hostile strangers.

"Maybe I should wait for him to show me," I hedge.

She's already out the door. "He won't mind."

She's very cute, but that doesn't mean she can't be very wrong. I go after her with every intention of stopping her, but when I reach for her arm, she's already turned the doorknob. Ben's room is a mess. Piles of folded laundry lean into each other on a chair. Books and boxes and papers hide what is probably a desk. There are football jerseys pinned to the wall over what look like years of team photos. His guitar rests against the open closet door. If Ben lived in a romance novel, his room would be full of riding tack, or locked cabinets full of state secrets.

Raquel wrinkles her nose. "It smells like *boys* in here."

"And something else," I add, not sure what to call it.

"That's Torpedo. Hi, boy," she calls, jumping onto the jumble of covers on the bed. I am so close behind her that I can actually see the cloud of dog hair billow toward me.

She snuggles her face into Ben's dog, and I hear him do a whimper noise that could either be anxiety or adoration. I'm guessing anxiety, because it looks like Raquel is about to love him right off the bed. I'm feeling a little anxious myself, and take an involuntary step backward—right into Ben, who chose this inauspicious moment to come looking for me (or Raquel, I guess).

"Hi, everybody," he says. The dog's head comes up, tongue out, at the sound of Ben's voice. I can see that he's old—creaky and gray. I didn't know dogs got gray hair, but here it is, all over my sweater.

"I was just showing Sarah around," Raquel tells him, relieving me from the panic caused by my intrusion.

"I'm glad you introduced her to Torpedo. I hate for him to feel left out." He's only talking to Raquel, and has managed not to touch me since I stepped into him a minute ago. Hands in his pockets, he looks around to assess the impression.

"Sorry about the mess. I've been told about seventy times that I'd better get it cleaned up or I'd be embarrassed." He shrugs. "I can't say that it's really bothering me." He sounds cool—not like as in Paul Newman cool, more like icy cool. Tuesday's relief about everything being all better is evaporating fast.

Raquel pats the bed beside her. "Come pet Torpedo," she orders me.

I sit stiffly on the edge of Ben's bed with all kinds of weird thoughts racing around my head, but none weirder than the memory of the last time I was this close to a dog this big. I force myself to touch him, and when he does nothing more terrifying than roll his yellowish eyes my way, I relax a little. Enough to stroke his back and the top of his head.

I'm not eager to start up a conversation with Ben, so I decide to tell Raquel a story.

"When I was a kid I hated going to my grandma's for Thanksgiving."

Her eyes go wide. "Really? Were you the oldest too?"

"Nope. It's because I have a cousin named Evil Evan."

"Is that really his name?" She's suspicious.

I decide to be honest, at the risk of lessening the effectiveness of my story. "No, that's not really his name, but it should be. He's just plain Evan. He is three years older than I am, and when I was five he thought it would be fun to see how long it took me to get dizzy and throw up. So he spun me around in my grandma's backyard. I walked into her yucky dead garden and tripped over a dry cornstalk. I was so mad, but I didn't cry, because Evil Evan would have loved that. So he sent another cousin inside for a dish towel. Then he blindfolded me and spun me again. That worked better for him, because I fell down faster, this time into mud."

Eyes wide, Raquel feels my pain. "Did you tell?"

I shake my head. "My grandma would not have liked to see me walk inside all covered in mud. So I acted tough and pretended it didn't bother me. Then Evan got his really great idea. He blindfolded me again and tied me to the dog. Grandma had this scary German shepherd with huge pointy ears and huge pointy teeth, and even before Evan tied me to it, I was scared to death of that dog. It dragged me all over the yard. I was screaming and tripping over lawn ornaments, and the dog was yelping and barking and I was sure it was going to eat me any second."

"Did it bite you?"

"No. Evan's dad heard me screaming and came out to rescue me."

"Was he mad? Did Evil Evan get busted?" Malicious vengeance dances in her eyes. How cute. She's protecting my honor.

"He was not mad. He thought it was hilarious and said something stupid about Evan being 'all boy,' which is code for 'really naughty and unable to obey.' Then he hosed me off and sent my aunt to find a sweatshirt for me to wear. I have been afraid of dogs and Evan ever since."

She looks up at me in surprise. "You're afraid of dogs? Really?"

I nod.

"But you're petting Torpedo," she argues, as if my dog fear was supposed to make sense.

I glance down at my hand, knuckle-deep in Torpedo's neck fur. "He probably isn't going to drag me around the yard or try to eat me. Besides, he feels good," I say, realizing that it's true. It feels nice to pet this warm, stationary, harmless dog. Ben's dog. The dog he loves and which is currently shedding ridiculous amounts of hair all over his room.

Ben walks around the corner of the bed and sits by Torpedo's head. The dog lifts his face slowly and rests it against Ben's leg. Raquel leans over on Ben's shoulder.

Realizing I am the only one in the room not allowed contact with Ben, I get off the bed and walk over to pick up the guitar.

"Can I?"

He gives me the barest nod—translatable as go-ahead-if-you-must.

I must.

Tuning only takes a second, and I realize he must have been playing this morning, before he came to pick me up. I start picking out the song he wrote, the one he played for me the first night we played together. It sounds so much better on his guitar than on mine. But my fingers fumble a bit on this perfect instrument.

"What's it called?" Raquel wants to know.

Ben looks at me, waiting for me to answer.

"It's Ben's song," I say. "He wrote it. He can tell you the name."

"It doesn't have a name. It doesn't even have words." He sounds a little disgusted. Does he remember that he once asked me to write words for him?

"Well, write some. A song should have words, you know."
Raquel's probably right.

"I don't do words," Ben says. "Maybe she'll write some one day."

He won't even say my name? And yeah, apparently he does remember that I never gave him words for his song.

"Ben?" His mom calls up the stairs. "Are you up there?"

"Yeah. What do you need?"

"Would you and Sarah come set the tables, please?"

"And Raquel?" Raquel shouts, eager to show her grandma that she's found her crowd.

I can hear the smile in Ben's mom's voice as she calls up, "And if you could find Raquel, I'd love her help, too."

As I place the Gibson back in its case, I watch Ben slide out from under the dog's chin. He kneels down on the floor so their faces are level and holds the dog's head in his hands, just looking at it for a minute. I've seen that look before. It's an adoring look, and once, he looked at me like that. Before I managed to ruin everything.

"Come on, Sarah. Let's go help my grandma set tables," Raquel says.

## Chapter Sixteen

Heading into the kitchen for plates and silver, I realize what's been missing from the house today. It doesn't smell like food. The kitchen smells pine-fresh and is perfectly clean, but there's no turkey scent, no burned pie juice on the bottom of the oven, no onions-and-celery smell from stuffing. Checking the clock in the kitchen, I discover that it's 3:00—far too late to start anything. I guess we'll be eating potatoes and not much else. Good thing I brought lots. And they're really tasty.

Ben's mom, wearing a spotless apron, is putting together a salad. And she's using a recipe. That makes me want to laugh, but I manage to keep it to a smile. Ben catches my eye, just for a second, and half-smiles back. But mostly he still looks like he's in pain.

*What am I doing here?*

*Invited.*

*Yeah, but he obviously regrets it.*

*True, but whether he's pleased to have you or not, this is where you want to be, isn't it?*

*I thought so, until the only person who will speak to me is six years old.*

*Seven.*

*Right.*

The doorbell rings. Ben's mom looks at the clock in alarm and then scoots out to the door. I walk into the dining room carrying a stack of plates; Raquel is on my heels with fists full of silverware. Heading back for another load, I cut through the family room, where all the adults are sitting. Immediate hush. Sneaky glances, such as the ones that scream *We've been discussing why Ben would bring a girl he hates to spend a family holiday with us.* I decide to smile, but it hangs in the air between us like a rejected flag of truce. Any minute the arrows are going to start flying.

I mutter, "Excuse me," as I walk between them, grateful for little Raquel protecting my back. In the hall I almost crash into Ben's mom, who is balancing a stack of square boxes and directing traffic with her head.

"Right through here, please. That's right, on the counter."

She nods to the guy in the hat and apron—the deli delivery boy, I realize—who is laden with trays and holding a bag over his arm. Hugging the wall, I stay out of the way as they pass and witness firsthand a never-before-seen holiday custom: Ordering in a turkey dinner.

The guy pulls a paper out of his apron pocket. Reading from it without looking up, he says in a humiliated voice, "Happy Thanksgiving to you, and thanks for letting Granny's Pantry be a part of your celebration. If you are planning to eat later than fifteen minutes from time of delivery, place all dishes covered in foil into a warm oven, and all dishes covered in plastic in a refrigerator. Enjoy your meal, and please call on us again." He turns and runs out the door.

Ben's mom snaps into action. "Ben, take this tip out to him before he gets away. Raquel, will you open up the fridge, honey? Let's put this food inside until we're ready to eat it."

I head back to the dining room, though not through the sea of resentful siblings this time. Sliding plates onto the table I allow myself one small smirk of amusement that Ben's mom either can't cook or chooses not to. No wonder he's so impressed with my food.

Suddenly the combination of deli dinner and discomfort strike full force, and I start to laugh. Not too loud, but it won't be kept in. I feel a small touch on my elbow, and spin around to see Raquel with her hands full of spoons. This, for some reason, is also funny, and I wrap her up in a hug. She looks up at me in surprise, maybe mixed with a little terror. Sliding to the floor, I sit down behind the table and try not to laugh too loud. She sits beside me, staring at my face as though I might be insane. She might be right.

"Um, Sarah? Are you okay?"

"Who knows? This is the weirdest day ever, isn't it?"

She shrugs. Apparently this is pretty standard for her.

"Okay," I decide to lay it all out for her. "Ben asks me to come here and then changes his mind. He'd like to uninvite me, but that would be rude. Instead he brings me to a house full of people who hate me and then he hardly says a word to me. I think I'd prefer the rude." I wipe a giggle-induced tear away from my eye. It feels really good to wipe that eye. I decide not to stop. Still rubbing, I continue.

"And there's a really big dog that I just might love. And we're eating take-out for Thanksgiving. That's great, of course. I'm not saying it isn't. But it's pretty weird for me." Rub, rub. Now both eyes need my attention. I sit on the floor next to Ben's little niece, rubbing the tears out of my eyes and no doubt doing all kinds of damage to my makeup. I don't even think about the damage I may be doing to my friendship with Ben until I hear him clear his throat at the doorway.

"Everybody all right in here?"

I try to stop rubbing my eyes, but it's like a magnetic force is attaching my hands to my face. I manage to pull my hands away, but I can't see Ben—or anything else for that matter. My eyes are swimming, and my eyelashes feel sticky. Imagining what I must look like, I laugh harder, and Raquel takes the matter into her own capable hands.

"Sarah's having a little breakdown. I'm sure she'll be fine. Want to help me set the table?"

Now that someone else is talking, I feel safe to let it out, and I laugh for real. I still can't see, or stop touching my eyes, and now I'm having a little trouble breathing. I feel Ben sit down next to me and he hands me a napkin. It's cloth, and I feel guilty wiping my eyes on it, but desperate times call for desperate measures and all that. I wipe my face and sneak a look at the napkin. Major tracks of makeup. And I didn't wear that much to start with. Which means I am most likely without any now.

"Are you okay?" he asks.

"I'm great. You're so sweet. Sorry about today. I'm sorry your family hates me, but I'll be polite and everything."

"No, I mean your hands," he says.

My hands? What about them? I look down to see that my fingers are sausages. Red, spotty, swollen sausages with fingernails.

"Eww. That's disgusting," Raquel and I say together, which

makes me laugh again, but only for a minute. Then I pull up my sweater sleeves and check my wrists. Covered in hives.

"Um, Sarah? You might want to come in here to the bathroom for a minute." Ben nods in the direction of the front hall. "Let's go through the kitchen," he adds in a moment of pure chivalry.

His mom is stacking boxes of pie on the counter by the sink. We slip past her and Ben ushers Raquel and me into the powder room. I only notice I'm rubbing my eyes again when Ben's hands gently push my fists off my face. He turns me to face the mirror and I gasp. Just like a shocked romance novel heroine. One whose face is swelling nearly beyond recognition.

"Is it possible," Ben asks, "in all the years you've been avoiding being tied to dogs, that you may have developed an allergy?"

"I'm not allergic to anything," I protest, with that unromantic whine in my voice.

And he laughs. Like he used to, before I screwed everything up. He laughs like life is actually funny, and he's glad to witness it with me. His arm even goes around my back, and he gives me a half-hug before he remembers that he doesn't do that anymore.

Kneeling down next to Raquel, he looks in her eyes and says, "Can you stay here with Sarah for a minute? Don't let her scratch anything. Maybe you could tell her a story or something. I'll be right back." And he plants a kiss on her head.

I catch a glimpse of my face in the mirror and know for sure that no one will ever kiss me again. My eyes have been replaced by red, splotchy golf balls. I can barely open my left one. I look like I've been in a biker fight. This wouldn't be funny even if it were happening to someone else.

*Well, maybe if it was happening to someone else.*

*No. Nobody could laugh at this.*

*You might if it was Existential Cousin.*

*No way.*

*Oh, be honest.*

*Okay, maybe I'd laugh a little.*

The thought makes me smile just enough to know that smiling makes the current situation worse. My cheeks have no place to go. They run into my huge eyes and sticky tears spill out. I lean over the sink to wash off my face, thinking that maybe I can rinse the offending dog hair out of my eyes. As I splash water onto my face, I feel Raquel's little hands pull my curls off my cheeks and forehead. She gathers my hair into a bunch against my neck and holds it there, out of the water.

The sweetness of her gesture has me feeling all tender. Until she says, "You have such pretty hair, Sarah. I love the boingy curls. You shouldn't let it get messy, especially since your face is so bad."

"Where is Uncle Ben?" Time to change the subject.

He walks in, nervous. "Hi. Okay. We seem to be all out of allergy medicine. I'm going to run to the drugstore and be right back. Are you two all right?"

"Can I come with you?" Raquel asks.

He looks at me. I wonder if he's planning to leave me all alone in this bathroom, while outside the door the jackals circle.

"Maybe we should all go." He grabs my hand and pulls me into the hall. Looking around like a spy in a movie, he searches for a clear path to the front door. No such luck. Siblings and cousins are now in full help-mode, wandering from kitchen to dining room, shuttling glasses and folding napkins.

He pushes us into the laundry room, whispers, "Wait here," and bolts back toward the kitchen. A minute later he returns, holding a set of keys that I've never seen before.

"Are you stealing a car to go buy medicine?" I ask. I can't decide if that's romantic or terrifying. Then I remember the state of my face and know for certain that romance is out.

"Come on, girls. Let's go." He leads us out to the garage and into his mom's car. Riding to the drugstore, I keep my visor down so I can stare at my reflection. Maybe if I keep looking at it, I'll appear less hideous.

*Not so much. In fact, I think it's getting worse.*

*Oh, come on. How much worse could it get?*

*Do you really want to know?*

Sighing in defeat, I close my eyes (an easier job than usual, since the lids are only open a tiny slit) and lean my head back. I feel Ben's hand in my hair, petting me, twisting a curl out of my face.

"Does it hurt?" he whispers.

Should I be honest? Or should I say what will make him feel better? "Mostly my pride, I guess. It stings a little, and feels kind of bruised."

"Sorry."

"Yeah, thanks. This will teach me to go uninvited into a guy's bedroom. You never know what's going to be lurking." I try to smile again, but the results are, I can tell, dismal. "You know what? How about you just take me home? I'll sleep this off and be fine tomorrow."

*Tomorrow? As in the tomorrow when you're scheduled to be on a fake stage in front of dozens—or maybe hundreds—of Chel's friends tomorrow?*

*Oh, life is hilarious.*

"No way. Somebody needs to take care of you. I really doubt your roommates are going to do it." He pulls into a parking lot. "You stay here. Raquel, come with me. We'll be right back.

154

Don't go anywhere." As if I'd dare. He leaves the keys in the ignition so the radio keeps playing. The thoughtfulness of that tiny gesture brings tears again to my swollen eyes.

*This is a great guy.*

*You think you need to tell me this?*

*Yeah, I know. But why is he being so weird? Earlier he was acting like he'd made a huge mistake, and now he's all back to normal—or abnormal, or whatever.*

*Does it matter? We need to fix this. Hang on tight. Give him a reason to come back around. You know—after the face is back.*

I close my eyes and press my palms against them. They feel like hot pillows, all puffed out and stinging. If a moment this ridiculous ever made it into a romance novel, the stupid swollen girl would have only two choices: either die in the arms of the man who would have loved her despite her disfigurement, or fall in love with the doctor who cured her.

I don't see either of those things happening for me.

After two more songs play on the radio, Ben and Raquel come racing back to the car. He cracks a cellophane wrapper off a bottle of allergy syrup and hands it over. I stare at it, uncomprehending.

"Drink it. I saw it in a movie once."

I take a sip. The sugar jolts me until the flavor takes over and induces a full-body twitch. "Oh, that's nasty."

"Drink it up."

"All of it?"

"I don't know. It can't hurt, can it?"

Is he asking me because he thinks I might know? I suppose it could hurt very much, especially if I throw it up all over his mom's upholstery. But my options are limited here. I tip up the bottle and suck it down. He stops me just as I'm about to spit up syrup.

"That's probably enough for now."

I try taking calming breaths to soothe the gag reflex. It's working, because I am feeling both calmer and less likely to make a mess. With my eyes closed, I feel him press a bottle into my hands.

"I don't think I can do the rest of it," I say, with a valiant effort to keep the whining out of my voice.

"It's water. I thought you might need to chase the medicine down."

Once again, his thoughtfulness makes me want to cry, or sigh, or something. "Thanks," I mutter. Gulping the water gives me a minute to get myself in control. I calm down enough to remember that I am completely hideous. Time to try again for an escape. "Will you take me home, please?"

"Sure," he says quietly.

Well, that was easy. Maybe too easy. He must have finally decided that putting me on display in front of his family is a bad idea. Maybe he's imagining the years of teasing ahead—"Hey, remember when you brought that scary girl to Mom and Dad's for Thanksgiving?" "Yeah, we hated her, didn't we?" "What ever happened to her, anyway?" "I heard her face exploded and she had to enter a convent so she could hide from the world."

I finish my water, but my throat feels tight. I wonder if it's swelling and closing, too. Will my airways constrict and suffocate me? Naturally the thought makes me panic. My heart beats faster. I lean over my knees and practice calm breathing. Then I feel Ben's hand on my back and I freeze in place. He rests it there, right in the middle of my spine. I can't breathe. Is my throat turning on me now, or am I just in way too close a proximity to Ben? Who knows? There's very little difference between pleasure and pain, here.

When the car stops, I open my eyes, ready to cheerfully thank him for taking me home, ready to act thrilled with the prospect of spending the afternoon alone, foodless and inflated. But I'm not home. Not at my home anyway. We're back at Ben's parents' house.

I look at him, forcing my eyes open against the afternoon sun. *Ouch.* "Um, I thought we were taking me home," I try lamely.

"Pretend you're home. I'm not going to leave you alone like this." He gestures to my head, which now feels roughly the size of a pumpkin. A big one. "Just one more thing before we go back in." He digs into the sack from the drugstore, pushing past more bottles of allergy medicine, and pulls out a pair of huge, square sunglasses. "You might want to wear these."

I cannot help it. The tears push past the softballs that were once my eyes.

"I told you she'd like the black ones better," Raquel says in a bossy voice, which, of course, cracks me up.

Laughing and crying and really wishing for a tissue and several minutes alone in a bathroom, I say, "No, these are great. I think they look perfect. Brown is my favorite color."

"Uncle Ben told me that. I didn't believe him. I didn't think anyone likes brown best." She shrugs and unbuckles her seatbelt.

"Can you tell Grandma we'll be right in?" Ben dismisses her, but she doesn't seem to mind. Bouncing out of the car, she slams the door shut and runs into the house.

Ben puts both hands behind his head and closes his eyes.

He looks as exhausted as I feel. He takes a deep breath and exhales for what seems like forever.

I put on the sunglasses and turn my head toward him. "Thanks. For the medicine and the water and the sunglasses and everything. That was great."

He doesn't open his eyes or turn his head. Is he trying to think of something nice to say? He had his opportunity to get rid of me and he didn't take it. I have no idea how to feel now, except grateful. I reach my hand out and put it on his arm, just below the shoulder. I can feel him tense up, but I don't know how else to show him that I appreciate what he's done, so I leave it there. After a couple of minutes, he takes another deep breath and turns to face me.

"Sorry about today. This isn't turning out like I'd planned," he says. He looks miserable. And gorgeous.

"You mean you didn't expect me to inflate like some psychotic balloon decoration?"

He tries to laugh and almost makes it. "I mean I'm sorry that you're uncomfortable. I wanted my family to see how great you are and everything. I guess they're not all being totally, um, receptive." He pauses, then adds, "They may have thought that things were a little different between us—you and me, I mean. Maybe they expected us . . . And they know that I told you about . . ." He's running out of steam. I can tell how weird he feels. Maybe the siblings thought we were Together, and they're disappointed that we're only friends. Or maybe they're shocked that he'd even want to be with me that much. Or maybe they're embarrassed that I know about the reading thing. I decide to lighten it up for him.

"What, are you kidding me? They love me. How could they not? They all want to be my new best friend. And Raquel's parents are definitely thrilled that she wants to hang out with me. They'll love it when she tells them that we had to sneak out and get me a hit of drugs before dinner."

He's laughing now.

"Thanks, Ben. For taking care of me." That sounded too scary. Too intense. Water it down, now. "You're a good friend."

He nods, but he's not laughing anymore. Looks like my intensity scared him away again. I wonder if I'll ever get this right.

"Okay. Ready?" he asks.

"Let's do this thing," I say with a fake smile of bravery.

As we walk into the house, I hear busy sounds of food passing from one room to another, glasses being filled, and all the general bustle of a major dinner production. Ben and I slip into the madness, picking up dishes and delivering them to the buffet table in the dining room. Coming around the corner with my hands full of cranberry sauce, I very nearly smack right into Krissy.

*Oh, the perfect day is now complete.*

*No, really. Could this get any better?*

*He could have given a little warning.*

*What is she doing here?*

"What are you doing here?"

I am relieved to discover that it was not me who said these words.

I paste on a passably sincere smile and answer her. "Hello, Krissy. Happy Thanksgiving. It's nice to see you, too."

"What's with the sunglasses? Are you going undercover?" she sneers.

I shrug and walk the cranberries over to the serving table.

Raquel, carrying plastic cups to the "little kids" table (for everyone younger than she is), sets down her load and attaches herself to my leg. "Kris, did you meet my friend Sarah?"

I try to ignore this next part, I really do. Because I know what's coming. But obviously I'm a glutton for punishment because out of the side of my eye, I watch Krissy lean her face toward Raquel's ear, shaking her head and whispering. Then Raquel moves her face away and shakes her own head. She moves toward me. I would fear the confrontation coming my way, but the buzz of antihistamine is dulling my discomfort enough that I figure I can stand on my own against Ben's cousin and his niece. I take a bracing breath and wait for Raquel's attack.

Walking up to me with all her seven-year-old importance, she slides close to my side and takes my hand. Her smile lights up her face as she squeezes my swollen knuckles. Through my over-the-counter drug-induced haze, I realize that this small person is choosing me. She wants to be my friend, despite (or maybe because of) the totally opposite reaction of the rest of the household. I squeeze back and we head to the kitchen for more deli dinner.

Maybe it's because Raquel's on my side. Or maybe because I really want to make things right with Ben. Or maybe it's the medicine, but I force myself to face Krissy and smile. It doesn't feel totally fake. I hold my spotty, itchy, swollen arms out for her to load me up. She slides a pan of green bean casserole into my hands.

"I'm watching you," she whispers.

"Okay," I nod. She looks surprised. But what else is there to say? I can't really attack her for being a girl without self-confidence, now can I? I've sort of parked myself on the corner of Insecure and Unsure. I know the territory. Just because we handle it in a different way, doesn't mean we can't see each other's points, right? I smile again, but she has turned away.

⌒⌒

I'd love to tell all about the dinner now. How the turkey and stuffing tasted, how the containers labeled "Granny's Pantry" felt under my fingers as I passed them on from my right (Raquel's eager hands) to my left (Ben's shoulder). I'd love to report the happy, ceaseless conversation, the lists of "gratefuls" and the casual jokes and laughter.

But I can't.

It's all lost in a haze. What I can remember, in disturbing distinctness, is trying through excruciating odds to keep my eyes open. The medicine and my puffed-out lids fight against my manners, forcing my eyes to become heavier and heavier as the evening wears on. When I am addressed directly (which happens very rarely), I force myself to smile and nod. This presses my cheeks against my sunglasses and causes my bruised-feeling eyes to water and my head to feel painfully near explosion.

Ben glances at my plate a few times, and I shove a few bites down. It's not like the food tastes bad, I'm sure. I'm just much too tired to chew. To swallow. To sit up in my chair.

*How long can this meal really last?*

*Feels like forever.*

*Ask him to take you home.*

*No. You ask him.*

*Too tired to speak. I'm just going to rest here.*

The next thing I remember is leaning forward in the front seat of Ben's Subaru, straining against the seatbelt at a stop sign. I look out the windshield and realize that we're only a few blocks from my apartment. My head weighs about half a ton, and gravity is working on it. Hard.

"Um." This is the best I can do?

"Good morning, again." He smiles just a little.

"Hi." Can I ask about the exit scene? Can I possibly want to know? "Did I thank your mom for dinner?" My tongue feels as thick as my eyelids.

"She got the message," he says.

I look over at him. Even through the sunglasses, it's painful to face the streetlight on the corner.

He pulls into the parking lot and my head thumps against the window. Ouch. Slipping smoothly into a stall, he brakes gently enough that I remain upright.

"Could you possibly just lay me down on the road and run over me a few times? I think I'd rather be roadkill than ever face you or your family again."

He almost laughs, but it comes out sounding pain-filled and exhausted.

*Maybe he drank the medicine too.*

"I think I'm sick," I try. Maybe starting from the beginning will help me unravel whatever is going on.

"You need to get to bed. You have a big night tomorrow."

He's not looking at me. Why isn't he looking at me?

"Yeah. You, too. The big night, I mean. I guess you can go to bed whenever you feel like it." My brain is whirring, but nothing—no thought, no action—is clicking into place.

"Should I pick you up for the party, or do you want to meet me over at Chel's?" He's very polite, except for the part about not facing me. But I can't really blame him, can I? I'm a scary, swollen narcoleptic.

I wish I knew what to answer. I think Chel expects me to

help set up. And I'm supposed to oversee some food business, if I can just remember what exactly. I really need to get out of this car. Because now, besides feeling like I'm about to explode and drop into a coma, I'm also ready to cry.

Ben, what's going on? What happened? All I want is for us to be back to normal. I want you to be the Ben you used to be— the funny, charming, attentive friend I've come to depend on. I want you to look at me, a little. But maybe not see my face as it is today. I want you to laugh again.

I should be answering a question right now, but I can't seem to remember what it is. Something about the party.

"I guess I'll see you there," he speaks for me.

"That's great. Thanks." I can't say anything else for a second, and that lame word hangs in the air between us. Deep breath. "Thanks for dinner, and for helping me out with everything." I gesture vaguely to my face.

He finally looks over at me and smiles that tooth-peeking grin. "Do you need help getting in?"

"I think I'm good. But really, thanks."

He nods at the steering wheel as I vault out the door.

## Chapter Seventeen

I sleep for fourteen hours. With nobody in the apartment and nobody calling or knocking, there's nothing to disturb me. Dragging myself out of bed at ten in the morning, I dare a glance in the mirror. Much improved. I decide to call my mom's cell phone.

"Hi, Mom. Happy Thanksgiving."

She yawns into the phone. "Sorry, hon. I was just on my way back to bed. Been shopping since four."

It takes me a few seconds to process this. Shopping since four? In the morning? "Who is this? Let me talk to my mother."

She laughs. "I got it all knocked out—the Christmas gifts are all bought and tucked away."

"Wait—are you home? What about your weekend trip to the sweat lodge thing? Didn't you go?"

"Cancelled. The chief came down with food poisoning, of all things. We didn't find out until late Wednesday night, and we didn't want to bother you."

"What possessed you to join the crazy masses of

consumers?" She's never gone in for the rushing-crowd business before.

"Christine talked me into it. She's a pro at the Black Friday stuff."

Black Friday? Why would anyone willingly position herself at an event labeled Black Friday?

"Who is Christine?"

"You remember Christine Chandler, don't you? Jesse's mom?"

Did my mother just punch me in the stomach? Because it sure feels like it.

Taking a moment to process this bizarre conversation, I recognize that my own mother is hanging out with . . . well, if her son is the Prince of Darkness, that would make her the Queen.

She's still talking. "We went over there for Thanksgiving dinner yesterday. It was so thoughtful of them to invite us, since they knew our other plans fell through. Jesse was home from school; he said to tell you hello. He looks great, like always."

Yeah. I'll bet. That scumbag. He schmoozed my mother. And she bought it.

Wait. Why is my stomach all twisty? I lie on the couch, forcing my heart rate back to normal. My hands are shaking, and starting to sweat. I hate that my body forgot how much we despise him. It's trying to go all swoony. Will. Not. Happen.

I so hate that guy.

"What was that?"

Shoot. I think I said that out loud. "Mom, you know that Jesse and I have issues. Complications. I'd really rather not hear how fabulous he is, if you don't mind."

"Oh, sweetie. I know that was weird, when you thought you were dating him. But you know how it is, he's just so . . ."

I let her trail off, because I really don't need to hear the end of that thought again. Once is enough to have my mom tell me that any guy is just too pretty for me. And hearing about how all my other wonderful talents make up for any beauty I may lack? I can pass on that part of the conversation, too.

"I'm really glad you guys had fun. Give Dad a kiss for me. Talk to you later." The forced cheer in my voice fools her enough that she hangs up.

I'm going back to bed.

The walls in Chel's living room are draped with twinkle lights. Candles float in glass bowls on every surface. Some neighbor, doubtless burly and rugged, has moved the couches out of the way, leaving space for way too many people to mingle.

The kitchen has been hiding me pretty well so far, but there's enough food set out for a lot more people than this house is likely to see. I can't really justify staying in here much longer. I lean against the fridge and take a few deep breaths before I brave the growing crowd. Turning the corner, I practically bump into Dean, who is guiding a very pretty and exotic girl in to find a drink.

"Hey, guys. How's it going?" I lean over and whisper to Dean, "Thanks for coming."

"Lila, this is Sarah. She's the entertainment."

She looks at me with her eyebrows up, as if waiting to be amused. She'll be standing here a while if she expects me to make her laugh. Although, I suppose I could tell her about yesterday's humiliations, and if she's the type who finds comedy in in other people's disasters, maybe she'll vote me on stage for "Stand Up, Sit Down."

"Hey, I worked a shift this morning." Dean's Mister Chatty now. "I think I figured out what the Boss doesn't want you all to know."

You all? He excluded himself from our little group pretty easily.

"Yeah? What?"

"When I came back from break, she had her nose in some paperback romance novel with a lady pouring out of a dress. You know, those tacky books for people who don't have real lives?" He smiles. He knows. He can't really know. But it sort of seems like he knows. "I never pegged her for one of that kind. But you never can tell, right?"

Shaking my head, I point out the tub of sodas and gourmet waters by the table and mumble my way out of the kitchen. The Boss, reading romance novels? I'm ashamed and embarrassed for her. And for me.

Tandy and Maura are here, leaning into a lumberjack-type guy whom Chel must have imported for atmosphere: wide shoulders, no visible neck, plaid flannel, and boots. I wander over and touch Maura's elbow. She turns and flings her arms around me, which our proper cubicle distance has never led me to expect, and shoves me over to Tandy. She, I notice, manages to keep one hand on the lumberjack's arm as she air-kisses next to my cheek and wishes me luck.

Luck?

Oh, yeah. I'm going to need it, and possibly very soon.

I wander around for a half hour before I see Ben walk in, clutching the Gibson and looking as nervous as I feel.

I wave when I think he's looking my way, but he doesn't

react. Sliding and squeezing my way through the mounds of people, I make it to his side.

"Hey, you're here." I am so clever.

"Hi, Sarah. You look good. You know, better. Than yesterday." He is stammering and nervous, and it is so adorable.

"Yeah, thanks. You cured me." I bump his arm with my elbow, hoping to make him smile. He pulls away from my touch.

"Where should I . . ." He wags his guitar between us.

"Mine's back there, in Chel's room."

Seeing us, Chel drifts over. How can she drift in a jammed crowd like this?

"Hi, guys. Are you ready to take the roof off this apartment?"

She's kidding, right? She wants us to play now? First? "What about the other guys?" I plead with my eyes for her to give me a stay of execution, but no deal.

"You go first, warm them all up. Then the other bands can do their thing." That's the nice way to say that the other bands can play music her friends will recognize and be able to dance to.

Ben's already walking over to the microphones and amps that are set up in the corner. I shoot Chel a desperate glance.

"Give him what he came here for, Sarah." She smiles.

"He came here to play songs on his guitar with all kinds of strangers listening."

She rolls her eyes. "Yeah. That's what I meant. And to be with you, dummy."

I stumble my way to Chel's room and grab my case. When I return, Ben has finished tuning up and holds out his hands for my guitar. He tunes me up without looking at me. I search out friendly faces in the room. Tandy and the lumberjack have claimed a corner of the living room wall; he leans his head over to capture every word she says. Maura grins at me from a folding chair and salutes with a half-empty water bottle. If I can't see Dean, is that a sign that things are going well with the exotic Lila?

Handing my guitar over, Ben starts to pick quietly. He readjusts the amps and picks again. I must look terrified, because I am. Ben's face melts a little from icy to room-temperature. He leans over on his stool and whispers into my hair, "Just pretend we're on the floor at your place. Nobody's listening, anyway." Then he smiles right into my eyes and I allow myself to feel lucky.

We play softly, and a few people stop talking to hear us. Maura is by far our biggest fan, staring right at us and smiling her black-lipstick grin. After a couple of minutes, Chel walks over and shoves the microphone stands under our chins. I hear myself, singing and playing with Ben, through the speaker monitor. We sound so good it makes me want to laugh, but just a little.

"Not bad," Ben whispers.

I nod and keep playing. Ten minutes. Dean and Lila emerge from the kitchen (maybe she was really thirsty) and move closer to the little stage. People are dancing, sort of. More like swaying while they talk to each other. Thirty minutes. Tandy and Lumberjack are glued to their spot in the corner, and I doubt she's hearing a thing besides him. This is going well. No problem. Ben's ready for his solo, so it's my turn for a beverage break.

I suck down half a water bottle before I remember that getting the hiccups right now would be a bad idea. I hold the bottle in both hands like a security blanket and casually move around to where I can see Ben's face. He's not likely to turn far enough this way to see me watching him, and besides, he's focused.

This is a new song he's been working on. I can hear harmonies in my head, and I regret that I haven't practiced it with him. We really do sound pretty great together.

His song ends, girls swoon, and it's my turn for a solo.

He holds the stool steady with his foot so I don't slip as I sit down. I want to tell him he was awesome, but I'm afraid I might throw up if I open my mouth. Glancing up at his face, I offer a small smile. It feels like an involuntary muscle twitch and must look like a grimace, because his head bows in defeat. I've seen him go from uncomfortable to almost normal to performance-perfect to nervous wreck all in one night. I have an almost over-whelming urge to jump off the stool and wrap him in a hug.

But there's this guitar on my lap and I'm supposed to be playing a song. My song. His song. The one he's never heard words for.

Fingers fumbling on the strings, I pick out the opening notes. It sounds so hideous that I play it through again. Better. I start to sing.

> *Birds are rowdy at my window.*
> *They must know something's changed.*
> *My heart is broken, cracked wide open*
> *Because I can't find you.*
>
> *Leaves are slipping to the pavement*
> *Slide and glide to rest again.*
> *Can't end this race to discover my place*
> *Until I find you.*
>
> *Traffic rushes past the corner*
> *Where I stand, dazed and alone.*

*Starting, stopping, wishing, hoping*
*Won't help me find you.*

*Raindrops wash across the window*
*Mirroring my falling tears.*
*Won't you find me? Can you find me?*
*I'll try to find you.*
*I will find you.*

People are clapping. That's fun. I let myself smile, ready to enjoy the moment, when I hear Ben's voice, harsh in the microphone. "We're all done. Next band will be ready in ten." He grabs my guitar out of my hands and shoves it into my stand. Pulling me around the corner into the quiet hallway, he gets right in my face. And not in a good way.

"What was that?" He looks angry. This was not part of the plan.

"Um, it was . . . the words I wrote to your song?" Is that really a question? Suddenly I have no idea what to say. Even how to talk at all.

"Are you just messing around with me? What am I supposed to think of that?"

I try to steady my voice enough to speak. I'm actually a little afraid of him, he's so intense. I want to escape, but apparently I want to stay more, because here I am. Deep breath. "I wrote some words for your song. I was kind of hoping you'd like it."

He looks like he doesn't understand what I'm saying.

I try again. "I'm trying to fix things with you, but I don't know how. I want us to be like we were."

He shakes his head, like he still doesn't get it. "Like we were when?"

171

How do I say this? "You know. Before we got all uncomfortable." I am so lame.

"Before you found out I'm a dumb jock?"

"Ben, that's not true. I know you're not dumb." I'm breathing
really fast, but I don't think any oxygen is getting to my brain. "I
don't care about the reading thing." Well, that wasn't really what
I meant. "I mean, it doesn't matter to me. It's not—"

"Hey, Sarah!" Dean finds us at this very wrong moment.
"You guys were fantastic. Hey, man," he says to Ben, "your song
was good."

Lila reads the situation more quickly and clearly. "Nice set,
you two," she says, and pulls Dean's arm so he follows her out of
the hall, a look of confusion on his face.

We're alone again, and Ben says, "You want it like it was
before I kissed you." This is not a question.

My heart takes a dive to somewhere near my knees.

"Well, isn't that what *you* want?" I can barely hear my own
voice. "You keep talking about being friends."

He shakes his head, and his hair slips over his eyes.

I lean back against the wall so I don't fall over from an ex-
cess of mortification (and a drugstore hangover).

"Sarah! There you are," squeals Maura. Ben turns toward
her and sighs. He isn't even trying for polite. "Hey, you must be
Ben. You guys sounded great." I can see Maura's eyes taking in
the rays of discomfort shooting between Ben and me. "Okay,
well, sorry I can't stay, but I've got to head out. See you next
week, Sarah. Bye, Ben."

Ben watches her walk away, then continues as if we hadn't
been interrupted. "For a smart girl, Sarah, you're clueless. This
*friends* thing has never been my idea. You've been telling me for

weeks now how *you* only want to be friends, but then you pull out that song."

Wait a minute. I've been saying I only want to be friends? Where is he getting that?

"Did you mean it at all? Any of those words? And if you meant it, what's all the let's-be-friends business?"

Just me, trying to hold onto him any way at all.

"And if the song wasn't for me, how could you spring it on me like that? I feel like I just got kicked."

Part of me wants to respond, but I'm having trouble processing his words. I focus on breathing in and out for a minute. When I'm pretty sure I can stand up straight and look at him and breathe and speak all at the same time, I give it a shot.

"Ben, I'm sorry. I don't know how to talk to you."

"Don't worry. If you use words that are too big for me, I'll stop you." He's angry, and hurt, and it's making him sound mean.

I feel like I got smacked. But I have to keep trying. "I want to make things right. Everything was so perfect with you, but it freaked me out. Like I was playing dress-up in someone else's life. And now I've managed to mess it up so much that I'm not sure who you are anymore. Here's what I meant." I take a breath and hope for the best. "I still want to be your friend. I want you to come around. I want to play songs with you. I want to study with you, and eat with you, and laugh with you."

He looks wrecked, sick. There's no color in his face, and his eyes look heavy with sadness.

I guess I can't make it much worse, so I might as well go on. In barely more than a whisper, I say, "But I want the rest of it, too. I want your arms around me. I want your fingers in my

173

stupid hair. I want to feel like I deserve you. And apparently I'm willing to sing about it in front of all these people."

He shakes his head. I've said it, and now he has to tell me that I'm all wrong for him. He needs to cut the strings, or whatever. This is in his hands now.

"So what do you think I should do?" he asks me. "If you don't believe I love you by now, I don't know how I can ever convince you."

Love?

I can't breathe.

He really said that, didn't he? And so now *I* have to decide. Really fast. Can I believe him? Do I trust him? Because why would he lie to me? Especially when it makes him so miserable? But why, why in the world, would it be true? Why would he ever choose me? What could there possibly be about me that he wants?

I shouldn't ask, I know I shouldn't, but I do. "But why?"

He huffs, frustrated. "Why what?"

"Why me? You could be with any girl . . ."

He shakes his head. "I don't believe you. For months I have followed you around like an annoying little kid. I have haunted your apartment. I have called you so many times that my fingers automatically dial your number whenever I pick up the phone. I eat all your food. I scare your roommates away. I wait outside your classrooms like a stalker, hoping you'll come out alone. I would absolutely fall down at your feet, if I thought you wanted any of that. I butt my head up against this wall over and over, every day, just waiting for you to take one step toward me."

(Note to self: Remember to tell Dean he was absolutely right.)

Why am I even pretending not to cry? I am the biggest jerk in the world.

"Sarah, you broke me. I couldn't tell what you wanted. You're not really mean, are you? But I never knew what to think. You let me think you liked me. We had fun together. But you never gave me any reason to think you were interested."

Is he serious? I can barely breathe. My head is pounding. Never gave him reason to think I'm interested? He must know he is the most amazing guy in the room, probably in the world. Who wouldn't be interested?

"I didn't think I could keep it up anymore. How long was I supposed to carry it, and do all of it by myself? It was exhausting, and all I wanted was any reason to keep working so hard. And then the whole reading thing came up, and I can't even pretend that I'm smart enough for you. So I let you off the hook. And you ran with it—being friends was just what you wanted. Fine, I could handle that. Whatever it takes to be near you. So I told my family that it wasn't my girlfriend coming to dinner, just my friend."

Oh. And it looked like I had just broken up with him. Got it. That explains the hostility, the defensive protection of the pack.

"Then you sing that song. I want more than anything to believe it's for me. But if it was for me, should I even have to ask?"

This seems like a good time to stop assuming Ben knows what I'm thinking. I have been living inside the world's largest miscommunication. It is time to say what I think.

"Ben, I am so sorry that I hurt you," I manage to squeak out between ratcheting breaths.

He ducks his head so I can't meet his eyes. I've seen that posture before, but never on Ben. Why does it look so familiar?

Oh, no.

That is exactly what Mandy looked like when the Faceless Wonder broke up with her. Defeated. Stunned. Dispirited. He thinks I'm trying to end something. Again. I put my hand out to touch his arm and he flinches away.

I shake off the nerves and take a big breath. "I have something to say to you that I wish I could have said months ago. I am crazy about you. I have never felt like this about anyone. You are everything I've ever wanted. I know I will never deserve you—even half of you—but I let myself get carried away in the fantasy. I have so much fun with you, but I'm always waiting for you to come to your senses and realize that you could do better. I have, from the day we met, expected the moment that you walk away. Because you ought to find a girl who matches you. You deserve someone beautiful, someone tall and graceful with silky hair. Someone stunning and fabulous and perfect. You deserve someone a million times better than me." I'm not sure what I expect him to say next, but I know I should give him a second to speak. Or escape.

"Sarah, shut up."

Well, I wasn't expecting that.

"Here. I'll make it easy. Yes or no?"

His face moves so quickly that I don't have time to answer him before he's kissing me, challenging me to make a decision. His mouth softens as I go limp against the wall. He pulls away, just enough so I can see his whole face as he says, "How about you just try to believe that you are the one I want?"

I force my arms to move. Placing my hands on either side of his beautiful, perfect face, I whisper, "You are amazing. You are wonderful. You are like a dream. And I don't want to wake up, because I want you here. I am insane over you. Everyone I speak to has to hear about you. They see me blush when I talk about My Friend Ben. But I could never dare call you anything more."

I can physically feel myself crossing a line. All my muscles are tensed. I'm ready to run. Or die. It's terrifying. But even if I end up humiliated and embarrassed later, it feels like the right thing to do right now. "My whole life I've wanted to be this girl—the kind of girl who could be your girlfriend. I've wanted to be part of that world where people get to be the heroes of their own stories. I've wanted that confidence that comes with belonging where I want to be. I don't have any reason to believe that we should be together except that you say so. It makes no sense to me except that it's what I've wanted forever. But you said you want it too. So I am going to believe you."

He shakes his head. Is he saying no? I think not, because his hands are in my hair, and he's leaning, slowly, closer. I tip up and reach for him, pulling his head toward mine.

Sometime later—minutes? hours? months?—I hear the band's amplifier shriek and we pull apart.

My hands are still on his face, but he's looking at me and smiling. His cheeks are bright again, and his eyes sparkle. Just like they used to, when he looked at me like this. I slip my hands into his hair, rise up on my toes, and kiss his mouth again. His arms come around my waist and he lifts me up, holds me. He nestles his face into the side of my neck, under my hair, and whispers my name. Over and over.

*Isn't Sarah the most beautiful word in the world?*

*You'd better believe it, sister.*

## Epilogue

When Mom says it, I assume she's kidding. Of course she has to be kidding, right?

"I'm so glad you're home that all I want to do is spend a few lazy days hanging around the house with you. Then if you want to make some pies, we can take them over to Christine's for dinner."

"Oh, you're going to the Chandlers for dinner?" I try for offhand, but I wonder if she can tell I'm a little hurt. Why would she plan that while I'm home?

"We all are, silly. I'm not leaving you home alone for Christmas Eve dinner."

Christmas Eve dinner in the company of the wretched Jesse James. How perfect.

We show up on their front porch, and I feel queasy. The last time I was here, I was packing homemade cookies, flirting on a plate. But my mother is all comfort in this place. As soon as Christine lets us in, my mom darts around like she owns the kitchen.

I slip the pies into an empty corner of the counter and duck out of the room. Maybe I'll hang out with the dads. I figure I can find them pretty easily. How hard could it be? I can hear the football game noises drifting through the house. Following the sound, I try to remember my dad ever watching football on Christmas Eve before. Things are changing all over the place, here.

Except that. Him. Standing with his arm slung up on the doorway, looking all fake-casual, as though he's been standing here all afternoon, facing away from the TV.

Objectively, I can say this. Jesse James is a handsome guy. He has good hair, if "good" means "messy-on-purpose." His tan is faded by this time of year. He's backlit from the huge TV, but I can see he's smiling at me.

And I feel nothing.

Absolutely nothing. I'm not turning to jelly. I don't have a swarm of stomach butterflies. I have no desire to check my hair, or my teeth, or my breathing.

I walk straight past him. "Merry Christmas, Jesse. Nice to see you." I sit by my dad's feet. Now I feel something, and I like it. I think it's called pride, or confidence, or relief. Whatever it's called, it feels good. Leaning back against my dad's knees, I smile at the thoughts in my head.

I am so over Jesse.

He has no power over me anymore. I don't even care that he said stupid, mean things about me once, or twice, or for a year. It doesn't mean those things were ever true, it only means that he was being stupid and mean. And I don't need that.

That is because I have something much better. Even better than a romance novel hero, I have a real hero. Not an outlaw, a gentleman. And he's coming to visit in two days. Right after the big Christmas party with his family, at which, he assures me, he will clear my name and make them all love me. I'd almost like to be there for that. Almost.

If my life were a romance novel, he'd come charging in on his big white horse . . . but then he'd be all sweaty and dirty, and for sure I'd be allergic to the dumb horsehair covering his clothes. Or he'd sweep into port on his pirate ship . . . but then there's the small problem that I have of not living anywhere near a port. Not to mention all the pirate-y unpleasantness, like plundering and bloodletting and general masculine showerlessness. Those things seem romantic in a story, until you really get a good look at the details.

It looks like I prefer reality—yes, reality has imperfections (but also toothpaste) and misunderstandings (but also the chance to make up). I'll take the reality that arrives not in a hot-air balloon or a chariot or a fighter plane, but in a rusty, colorless Subaru with no radio.

This is my new reality, where I'm good enough to be with Ben, and nobody has to be perfect, and together we create our happy.

*Acknowledgments*

Sometimes I think writers write alone. Until I write something. Then I remember—this couldn't happen without loads of help. This story started for a conference. With helpful suggestions from that conference, and the critique group that grew out of it, it became a whole book. Thanks to my kids for thinking I'm not too out of touch, to Shelley Oudekirk and Deren Hansen and Annie Valentine, and especially to Annie Douglas, Emily Manwaring, and Pat Martinez for many, many readings. I borrowed several things for the philosophy class from the Web site from Lander University in South Carolina (lander.edu), because my college philosophy class was never quite as memorable as Sarah's.

Thanks to the whole gang at Shadow Mountain: Chris Schoebinger, Heidi Taylor, Lisa Mangum, Richard Erickson, Rachael Ward, and Sheryl Dickert Smith.

And, as ever, this one would never have made it outside my head without the support of the world's greatest husband, Scott. (Sorry, girls—he's taken. Forever.)

Scott Wilhite 2009

# About the Author

Becca Wilhite often gets just what she wants. Often, but not always. She loves the ocean, but lives in the mountains. Too bad. She loves the rain, but lives in the desert. Too bad, again.

She loves books, bookstores, libraries, and classrooms where there are stacks and piles of books. And she gets to spend hours every day with words and books. How lucky!

It's not much of a secret that she hears voices in her head. Sometimes they tell her good ideas for stories. Sometimes they tell her she's brilliant. Sometimes they tell her they want cinnamon bears. When she ignores the voices, they start arguing with each other . . . in British accents. Maybe she should listen to them more carefully.

Becca lives in a happy home with her near-perfect husband and four above-average children. You're welcome to visit her any time at BeccaWilhite.com.